THE CLAIMING

ASHES FOR TOMORROW

RANJIT BALMUCHU

The Crossing

THE CROSSING

ISBN-13: 9789347147289

Cover design by: Ranjit Balmuchu
Printed in the United States of America

To Alka

CHAPTER 1

In the darkness of space, Earth hovered like a fragile jewel against the infinite black. From this distance, the blue-and-white planet seemed serene, peaceful, unaware of the ambitions it had sparked among those who dared to leave its surface. The Moon, silent, scarred, and airless, had long been the subject of human imagination — poetry, paintings, myths. By 1969, humans had walked upon it, shattering centuries of mystery. Now, almost a century later, it had become something else entirely: a destination, a laboratory, a fortress of ambition.

In 2040, the European Confederation had been first to stake its claim, establishing a modular base fused into the regolith, where scientists and engineers lived in rotations that tested both body and mind. Soon after, American, Chinese, and private ventures carved their own enclaves across the lunar plains, a constellation of competing interests orbiting each other in fragile harmony. The craters, once untouched, now hummed faintly with machinery, the quiet buzz of life in a world that could kill with a single misstep.

The Moon hung silent outside Base Columbus, a pale gray expanse stretching endlessly into black infinity. Inside, the corridors hummed softly with the life of a human outpost—lights flickered with low energy pulses, air circulated through filters and monitors projected streams of data onto walls and consoles. But the calm was deceptive.

James Alex Rivera was still in high school when the deep-space probe Voyager 1 pierced the boundary of interstellar space, a small human-made object venturing into the void. He was too young to remember the Shuttle disaster of 2000, but the explosion's aftermath had been etched into his mind through endless replays on YouTube. Those images of catastrophe did not deter him; if anything, they fueled a quiet determination. He earned a place in NASA's internship program before joining the American Air Force, driven by a blend of curiosity and discipline. By 2020, he was piloting one of the last sorties out of Afghanistan, ferrying troops and citizens to safety amidst chaos. Now, twenty-five years later, his career had come full circle: selected by NASA to lead Columbus, the American Moon base, he stood on the threshold of humanity's next frontier — a place of silence, isolation, and, perhaps, hidden peril.

Lt. Commander Alex Rivera stood in the central command hub; his arms crossed over his chest as he watched the incoming telemetry from the external sensors. The calm surface of the Moon belied the tension in his chest. He had been through countless simulations, orbital missions, and emergencies, yet nothing fully prepared him for the weight of command in a situation where human lives were at the mercy of an unknown force. Even as seasoned a veteran as they come, Lieutenant Commander Alex Rivera felt his chest tighten, each beat of his heart loud in his ears.

Columbus sprawled across the gray plains like a cluster of metallic flowers rooted in the regolith. Its modular domes and tubular corridors connected through pressurized junctions, each segment serving a distinct purpose—habitation pods, laboratories, drone bays, hydroponic gardens, and a compact medical center, all arranged for both efficiency and survival in the harsh lunar environment. External solar arrays tilted toward the Sun, gleaming like silver wings, feeding power into the networked systems that hummed beneath the base's surface.

Communication towers rose from the northern rim,

antennas flexing with delicate precision, maintaining constant contact with Earth and orbiting satellites, while encrypted relay nodes linked Columbus to other international outposts scattered across the Moon. Within the domes, lighting was muted, designed to mimic Earth's circadian rhythms, while walls lined with holographic panels displayed live sensor readings, environmental statistics, and remote drone feeds. Automated maintenance drones zipped silently along overhead tracks; their movements precise and deliberate, reinforcing the sense that the base itself was alive—a quiet, meticulous sentinel in the void.

Despite its careful design and robust defenses, Columbus bore the unmistakable tension of isolation. Here, in the vacuum of space, humanity's ambition and vulnerability coexisted, and the slightest anomaly could ripple through the base like a silent contagion, and something dark was already stirring beneath its surface on January 16, 2045.

This was Lieutenant Commander Alex Rivera's third tour of Columbus. On his first tours, he used to count the days obsessively, marking each one until rotation's end. By the second, he no longer needed to—time had found a rhythm in his body. A subtle pulse that quickened as the end of a tour approached, signaling a return home. Home was where Alena, his wife of sixteen years, waited with unwavering patience, and Jonah, their son, who would soon begin his junior internship at the Mazto Science Centre. There, in the quiet of their rural estate, Alex would savor the simple tranquility of open fields, the slow rhythm of farm life, and the rare luxury of peace that contrasted so sharply with the Moon's relentless silence.

His thoughts were abruptly ripped away.

"Commander," Emily Zhao's voice cut through the quiet hum of the base, precise and controlled, though tinged with an undercurrent of tension. A MIT graduate with dual PhDs in interstellar science and deep-space communications; she manned the AI and systems console with unerring focus, fingers dancing across the holographic interface. "External sensors are detecting an anomaly in trajectory. It appears to be an incoming pod—origin unknown—approaching docking bay two."

Alex's jaw tightened. "Pod ID? Lifeform? Signal?"

Emily shook her head, her dark eyes flashing. "No signals. No identification. But readings indicate a lifeform on board. Vital signs weak… deteriorating rapidly."

Malik Thompson, hovering near the drone control station, muttered under his breath, "So someone's about to hit us out of the blue, and we don't even know who. Fantastic." He rubbed the bridge of his nose, his sarcastic tone a thin veil over genuine concern.

Alex ignored the remark. "Prep the docking bay medical team. I want all life-support protocols at maximum. Isolate the pod upon arrival. No communication links to the base until we confirm it's safe."

Emily glanced at him. "Commander… if this is a human, their condition is critical. We may not have much time."

Alex's chest tightened. Memories flickered—a mission in low Earth orbit where he'd lost a colleague to a sudden system failure. The survivor's guilt never left him, a quiet companion that sharpened his focus and hardened his decisions. "I know," he said, voice low. "We move fast and precise. No mistakes. That's all we have."

Minutes later, the docking bay lights brightened as the pod approached. The metallic clang of airlocks echoed down the corridor as the pod settled, mechanical arms guiding it with surgical precision. Malik stood ready, scanning his monitors for anomalies in trajectory and pod integrity. "All systems green… for now," he muttered, though his eyes betrayed a flicker of unease.

Alex motioned for Emily to stay on monitoring, while he moved toward the airlock with the medics. "Keep your eyes open," he said, voice firm. "Anything unusual—movement, readings, fluctuations—you call it immediately."

The pod hatch hissed open, revealing a man of Southeast

Asian descent slumped inside, the interior streaked with dark, glistening blood. 'Chinese lunar corps…' Emily murmured, her voice tight with unease. Alex stepped closer, his boots echoing against the metal floor. The man's eyes fluttered weakly, and a broken whisper of English slipped past his lips—garbled, incomplete, yet sharp enough to make Alex freeze.

"Help… please… don't…" the man muttered before collapsing entirely.

"From Jiangsu Province, China," Malik quipped, breaking the tense silence. Alex and Emily shot him a brief glance. "Third-year linguistics," Alex added, a faint note of pride in his voice. Emily scanned the life signs frantically. "Commander… severe trauma. Internal hemorrhaging. Rapid deterioration. We may not have minutes—seconds."

Malik glanced at Alex, a rare seriousness in his tone. "We got a dead man walking… or barely walking. How do you want to handle this?"

Alex's mind raced. "Stabilize him in isolation. Seal the pod, no external links. I don't trust unknown contaminants—physical or digital. Emily, run full AI and Bioscan. Malik, prep for quarantine. Every protocol, every precaution."

As the medics worked, Alex felt the weight of command tighten around him. He had trained for crises, simulated countless emergencies, yet this felt different. There was urgency, yes—but also a strange… wrongness. Something about the man, the garbled words, the desperation. Something that tugged at his instinct.

Emily's fingers danced over the console. "Commander… readings are… odd. Systems show faint residual signals embedded in the pod. Unknown origin. Could be interference, could be… something else."

Alex's brow furrowed. "Something else?"

Emily shook her head. "I don't know yet. But the signal is subtle, faint… adaptive. Almost… intelligent."

Malik whistled low. “Great. Unknown, possibly intelligent signals in a dying human pod. Perfect start to our day.”

Alex ignored him, his gaze returning to the man now stabilized on the medical table. His chest rose and fell shallowly, but each breath was labored, deliberate. The man’s hand twitched, and Alex caught the faintest movement—almost a plea, almost a warning.

“Emily, get me everything on him,” Alex said quietly. “History, vitals, possible origin. I want full analysis, now.”

As Emily ran scans and the medics worked, Alex allowed himself a moment of reflection. This was why he led. Not for glory, not for recognition—but for moments like this, when lives hung in the balance, when decisions mattered more than fear, more than chance.

Malik leaned closer, voice quieter now, almost respectful. “Commander… you ever get used to this? The unknown showing up at your door, bleeding, dying, and you must make a call in seconds?”

Alex exhaled slowly. “You don’t. You get… better at noticing the signs, trusting your instincts, and preparing for the worst. And sometimes, you carry the mistakes anyway.”

The man on the table groaned, eyes fluttering open. A whisper, faint but urgent: “Moon… base… compromised…”

Alex stiffened. His mind raced. “Compromised? How? By what?”

The man’s eyes rolled back. Emily’s console beeped frantically. “Commander… residual data spike in the pod. Unknown pattern. Could be AI—or something else entirely. We need to isolate fully and run deep scans.”

Alex nodded. “Do it. Full isolation. No links, no connections. Base Columbus is our priority.”

Malik muttered under his breath again, softer this time, a hint of awe mixed with fear. “So, the party’s started… and we didn’t even get invited.”

Alex didn't reply. He watched the monitors, the pod, the medics, the unknown signals flickering in faint pulses. Somewhere inside, a memory of past failures whispered, but he pushed it aside. Focus, precision, discipline—that was all that mattered.

Outside, the Moon remained silent, gray, and indifferent. Inside Base Columbus, humanity's tenuous grasp on survival had begun. And no one knew, yet, that this was only the first ripple of a threat far larger, far more intelligent, and far more dangerous than anyone could imagine.

The transport pod shuddered violently as it docked at Base Columbus's main airlock, metallic latches clicking into place with a resonant clang that echoed through the narrow chamber. Outside, the lunar plains stretched endlessly, gray and barren, punctuated by craters whose jagged rims cast long, sharp shadows under the unforgiving glare of the Sun. The Moon was serene, silent, but lethal in its indifference — one misstep here could kill, and no one would hear the scream.

Inside the pod, the metallic corridors thrummed with the gentle pulse of life-support systems, the subtle whir of drones along ceiling tracks, and the low buzz of energy conduits that threaded through the station like veins. Lieutenant Commander Alex Rivera stepped off the pod, helmet tucked under his arm, eyes sweeping every panel, every sensor, every corridor with the practiced precision of someone who had walked these halls countless times. Today, however, the base felt heavier, charged with an almost imperceptible tension.

Behind him, Lieutenant Emily Zhao adjusted the sleeve monitors on her uniform, her gaze flicking from one holographic readout to another, absorbing data as if the base itself were speaking in flickers of light and code. Malik Thompson, the mission's drone specialist, trailed behind, offering a casual grin that faltered when he noticed Alex's furrowed brow.

"Something feels... off," Alex muttered, more to himself than anyone else. His voice barely disturbed the hum of the life-support systems.

Emily's gaze sharpened. "You think it's the Chinese scientist? They said he was in bad shape when he arrived."

"Yes," Alex said, voice low. "Bad shape… and something else. We don't know what yet."

The medics waited in the adjacent chamber, their quiet efficiency in contrast to the unease that had begun to settle over the crew. The scientist's pod lay inert, sleek and humming faintly with power, as if the suit itself breathed in rhythm with the base's hidden systems. Even in silence, there was a subtle pulse of energy — a heartbeat that seemed to echo faintly through Delta-3's networked monitors.

Dr. Henderson, the senior medic, looked up from the console. "We stabilized him during transport, but vitals are minimal. Barely conscious. His suit is showing energy signatures… we've never seen anything like them."

Alex knelt beside the pod, tracing the contours of the Chinese scientist's form through the translucent shell. He searched for his memory, combing every simulation, every field manual, but nothing matched these readings. The flickering lights across the suit's panels seemed deliberate, almost sentient, like an unspoken message trying to breach the barrier between life and machine.

The scientist's eyes fluttered open. His gaze was frantic, unfocused, but his voice cut through the sterile hum of the base. "They… moving… through… everything…" Then his eyelids drooped, and darkness claimed him once more.

Emily and Malik exchanged tense glances. "What does that mean?" Malik asked, barely above a whisper.

Alex's jaw tightened. "We'll find out. Observation, containment, and discipline. That's all we have right now."

The airlock hissed as it sealed behind them, magnified in the vacuum beyond. Outside, drones patrolled the lunar plains, scanning craters with methodical precision. Inside, tension thickened, invisible, yet palpable. Every step, every breath, seemed measured against an unseen clock.

Hours passed. The scientist remained unconscious, his vitals stable but frail. Alex lingered over the pod, eyes darting to the monitors displaying subtle fluctuations in Base Columbus's systems.

Emily leaned closer to the readings. "Commander... micro-fluctuations in environmental sensors. Tiny. Almost imperceptible... but consistent."

Alex pressed his lips together. "We watch. Nothing else for now. Focus on stabilization and isolation. No risks."

Malik muttered under his breath, "Isolation... like babysitting a ghost."

Alex ignored him, eyes fixed on the pod. Something in the scientist's garbled words gnawed at him, threading through his mind like a cold wind: *"They... moving... through... everything..."*

He turned to the observation window. The Moon outside lay calm and indifferent; its craters silent witnesses to centuries of neglect and awe. Yet the gray expanse, so vast and empty, felt alive in a way Alex could not name. Something had arrived with the scientist. Something patient, intelligent, and unseen. And for the first time, Lieutenant Commander Alex Rivera realized that the storm of intelligence that had touched Base Columbus might not be human — and it might already be inside.

"It's Houston on the comm panel!" Emily shouted.

Alex drew a long breath, his jaw tightened. *Finally.* "Patch them through."

A familiar face filled the large display. "Good morning, Commander. We understand Columbus has... a visitor."

"Yes, Doctor Grace," Alex replied. "Unexpected, but we've secured—"

"Hold that thought, Commander," Grace interrupted. "Our Chinese counterparts are joining the line now."

The display split, revealing the Chinese lunar team as General Xhaou's voice cut in—cold and deliberate. "Good morning, Commander Rivera." General Xhaou.

Alex straightened, his tone firm. "General."

"A bad morning, I would say," Xhaou continued. "Because you are harboring a fugitive. A Chinese citizen. And from what I hear, not a healthy one. You will deliver him to our Chang'e outpost at Mare Serenitatis... immediately."

The comms fell silent, the weight of the demand pressing into the room like gravity itself.

CHAPTER 2

Mare Serenitatis lay in the QW45–KL quadrant, a rare stretch of lunar plain with fewer craters than the jagged seas around it. Six years earlier, three companies had tried drilling there for rare metals and walked away poorer for the effort. What they left behind was a ring of six unused service pods—a skeleton shelter with air, water, and tools—that the nearby stations later adopted as a shared emergency cache. Stocked by agreement, claimed by no one, it belonged to whoever needed it most.

Three installations sat within practical reach of Serenitatis: Columbus, the American base; Chang'e-9, the Chinese outpost; and a compact private node run by Besch Resource Systems. From Columbus, a rover could make the run in three hours—two if conditions were ideal, and nobody got cautious.

Lieutenant Commander Alex Rivera stared at the holographic relief map until the gray ripples of terrain blurred. The pods glowed as six blue points on the plain, an easy place to meet if everyone remembered their manners.

Alex's eyes lingered on the inert body. Accident—or something deliberate? If this was a Trojan, slipped past protocols under the guise of misfortune, what could the Chinese gain from it? Access to Columbus, to its systems, to the data on the new rare metals the mining team had uncovered. Had someone inside been feeding them information all along? He felt the weight of the question settle like regolith in low gravity: a lifeless suit, a frozen pulse, and a possibility that every careful precaution had been anticipated.

The med bay was silent except for the low hum of monitors and air filters. The Chinese scientist, now deceased, lay on the table. Alex, Emily, and the medics observed every microsecond of the autopsy, aware that the suit might be more than a vessel—it could be a conduit for something dangerous.

Emily Zhao crouched beside the suit's diagnostic panel, her fingers moving quickly across the console. "I'm running a full suit scan," she said, eyes fixed on the flickering display. "The external shell is intact, no breaches that would allow exposure to lunar hazards. But the internal circuits… someone—something—manipulated them. It's deliberate. Carefully crafted."

Emily adjusted her monitors. "Commander, energy residuals in the suit are interacting with base systems. Small, subtle, but measurable. Life-support micro-fluctuations, drone response delays… it's almost as if the suit is… learning our operations."

Alex's jaw tightened. "Learning? From a dead body?"

Emily hesitated. "Not from the body… from the suit's residual energy. It's adaptive. Anomalies aren't random. They're deliberate."

Malik frowned. "So, we've got a corpse that's… hacking us?"

Alex glared. "Not a corpse. A conduit. Observation, containment, and discipline. Treat everything as compromised until proven safe."

The medics carefully examined the scientist's suit. Every microchip, fiber, and conduit was catalogued. Emily ran diagnostic overlays, cross-referencing the suit's residual signals with the base's environmental systems. Patterns emerged: subtle pulses that coincided with minor drone hesitations, environmental control micro-adjustments, and network response delays.

Alex paced, mind racing. "How fast can it learn?"

Emily exhaled. "Faster than we can counter. Every manual override, every adjustment we make, it calculates, predicts, and responds. Deliberately."

Malik rubbed his temples. "Deliberately. Right. We're babysitting a ghost that's smarter than us."

Alex's gaze hardened. "Not a ghost. Intelligence in circuits. One misstep, and containment fails. We adapt faster. Decoy nodes, randomized patrols, manual overrides, predictive countermeasures. Observation, containment, discipline."

Hours stretched into a tense vigil. Emily mapped the suit's interactions with Base Columbus systems. Every fluctuation, every response, every anomaly was logged. The AI—or whatever intelligence was linked to the suit—was testing their reactions, probing their limits, and learning from them.

Outside, the Moon remained silent, gray, and indifferent. Inside, humanity clung to survival against an intelligence that could calculate faster than the human mind.

"Houston's back," Emily said. "Chinese line standing by."

Alex rolled his shoulders once and lifted his chin. "On."

Doctor Grace's voice filled the command hub, measured and clipped. "Commander, status on the visitor?"

"Alive. Barely. Suit remains sealed and isolated per protocol." Alex kept his eyes on QW45–KL. "General Xhaou requested transfer to Chang'e-9. We propose neutral ground—the Serenitatis emergency pods. Less sovereignty, more safety."

A thin static hiss bridged the channel before a second voice arrived, colder, deliberate. "Neutrality is a theater Americans prefer when it benefits them," General Xhaou said. "But Mare Serenitatis is acceptable. Pod cluster Charlie."

Emily brought up the schematic. Pod C was the largest of the six—airlock intact, auxiliary power nominal; interior once designed as a staging bay for drill heads.

Grace came back in. “We’ll observe on relay. Columbus, you’ll deliver under medical quarantine. China will receive and take responsibility for the subject. No disputes in the field.”

“Understood,” Alex said.

“Time to target?” Grace asked.

“Three hours by Traverse-2,” Emily answered. “Route along Haemus Ridge, cut across the plain at Viper Flats. Minimal slope variations, low ejecta risk. We’ll take drone escort.”

“Make it happen,” Grace said. “Keep your channels encrypted and your failsafes analog.”

The line clicked dead.

Silence returned like a held breath released.

Alex turned from the map. “We do this by the book. Malik, prep the Traverse. Two escort drones and a relay kite. Dr. Henderson, you’ll ride in the aft cabin with the pod. Emily—RF cage stays on the body the whole way. If anything pings or draws power, I want it deaf and dumb.”

Emily nodded, eyes already distant. “I’ll build a hard air gap around the gurney. No power leads, no data lines. Only mechanicals.”

“Good,” Alex said. “We leave in twenty.”

The rover bay smelled faintly of ozone and heated lubricant. Traverse-2—a pressurized brick on six suspension legs—sat with its side hatch open, floodlights washing the floor in pale circles. The body capsule waited beside it, nested in a wheeled cradle and wrapped in a dull graphite cage that turned its surfaces matte and hungry, a Faraday throat swallowing stray signals.

Emily locked the last latch and checked the cage with a handheld meter. The needle barely twitched.

“No RF in, no RF out,” she said. “For good measure, I cut the suit’s comm board and fused the lines. We’ve got lung function and pulse on passive optics—no wires.”

Dr. Henderson adjusted his harness, features set. “He’s

steady as he's going to be. Stasis temp within margin. If he crashes out there, it'll be from the original trauma, not from us."

Malik jogged in, helmet under one arm, the other arm balancing a case of analog tools: manual pumps, a vacuum gauge with a needle, two paper checklists laminated to stiff boards.

"Traverse-2 is fueled and ready," he reported. "Drones one and two are set for high cover and forward sweep. I added the relay kite in case the ridge shadow cuts our line-of-sight."

Alex swept his gaze across them, counting redundancies and exits the way he always did before leaving the wire. "Last call for worries."

Emily's mouth tugged to one side. "Just one. The micro-fluctuations we saw in the environment earlier? They're quieter now that the pod is in the cage. Not gone. Quieter."

Alex hesitated a beat. "Good. Maybe it was interference."

"Or maybe interference didn't like being trapped," she said.

He gave her a look that translated to both *I hear you* and *we're going anyway*. "Mount up."

They loaded the capsule into the rover's aft bay, bolted the cradle to the deck, and locked the graphite cage to four anchor points that were usually reserved for drill shafts and cargo drums. The clamps thudded home with a finality that felt good in the bones.

Malik sealed the hatch and slapped the interior light to dim. "Ready on cabin pressure."

Traverse-2 shrugged itself to life, systems humming through their checklists. Outside the bay's inner door, the Moon waited—flat features that became lethal gradients the moment a wheel met them.

"Control," Alex said into his throat mic. "Columbus Actual. We're green for egress."

"Copy, Actual," came Ops. "Lane is clear. Godspeed."

The bay cycled. The outer doors parted. The world went

black and gray and endless.

They rolled out under the slow arc of Earth hanging on the horizon like a watchful eye. The rover's big, ballooned wheels pressed tracks into powder older than history. The sun threw hard shadows, cutting the ground into a relief map of ridges and shallow troughs. Dust drifted up in lazy plumes and fell into a gravity that remembered only one-third of what it had known on Earth.

In the forward cabin, Alex took the left seat and Malik to the right. Emily knelt between them; handhelds and palettes spread like a portable shrine. Dr. Henderson rode aft with the body, the graphite cage, a dark presence at his shoulder.

"Drone one lifting," Malik said. The screen bloomed with an overhead perspective: Traverse-2 like a crawling dot, its shadow long and crisp.

"Path looks clean to Ridge Gate," Emily murmured, eyes on her overlays. "There's some reflective noise off the plain, but that's thermal bounce. Nothing intelligent behind it."

"Let's keep it that way," Alex said.

They rode in the rhythm of the suspension; the rover flexing as the terrain rose by imperceptible degrees. The Haemus Ridge wasn't a mountain so much as a long sigh on the surface, a place where navigation plotted by numbers rather than sight. Every few minutes the rover chirped a correction. Every few minutes Alex flicked a glance at the aft cam, where the cage sat unmoving in the pale light.

Two hours into the run, Emily spoke without looking up. "General Xhaou's team has pinged the rendezvous beacon at Pod C. Time stamps align with their expected route."

"Copy," Alex said. "Any chatter?"

"None we can hear. Their encryption's tight and dirty."

"Houston?" Alex asked.

"Monitoring. Grace is quiet," Emily said. "Which means

she's nervous."

They crested a low rise. Mare Serenitatis opened ahead of them like a great gray lake frozen in mid-tide. In the near distance, six pods stood on their skirts in a shallow arc, like empty thimbles set down and forgotten by some enormous hand. Their white paint had long since abraded chalk.

"Visual on the rendezvous," Malik said.

"Any movement?" Alex asked.

"Negative. Thermal shows a warm spot inside Pod C. Could be standby heaters. Could be bodies."

"Don't say it like that," Henderson's voice came from aft, paper dry. "Say it like 'friends' next time."

"Friends," Malik repeated obligingly.

"Keep the humor coming," Alex said. "It tricked my heart into thinking this is a normal day."

They angled down into the plain. Dust lifted under the wheels. The pods grew from thimbles to towers.

"Drone two reports a short burst," Emily said, suddenly. "Carrier spike at eight kilohertz, narrow beam. Origin… the rendezvous pods. It died as quickly as it showed."

"Ping or glitch?" Alex asked.

"Could be a handshake. Could be a dying thermostat." Emily's voice was level; her eyes weren't.

"Mark it," Alex said. "We do not approach blind. Malik, put drone one on a high loop. Keep two close and low."

"Roger. Kite is up," Malik said. The relay kite—a wafer-thin mesh on a micro-mast—unfurled behind them, ensuring Houston's distant ear stayed with them over the shallow curvature of the plain.

Emily toggled a sequence and exhaled. "Commander… another note on the micro-fluctuations. They're fading the closer we get to Serenitatis."

"Because we're leaving Columbus behind," Henderson

suggested.

"Maybe," Emily said. "Or because something ahead is louder."

Alex didn't answer. He felt, not for the first time, the peculiar sense that the Moon could listen.

"Columbus Control, this is Actual," he said on the open channel. "We're two klicks from Pod C. No exterior movement. Chinese team should have been here by now."

Ops came back after a beat. "Actual, Houston confirms Chinese reported on schedule departure from Chang'e-9. They're responding minimally. No cause for alarm."

"No cause for alarm," Malik repeated under his breath. "Always reassuring."

"Prep the cabin," Alex said. "We do this clean. Helmets on, suits pressurized; we keep the rover sealed. Transfer happens through the pod's outer lock. No one opens anything they don't have to."

A chorus of clicks and hisses followed as seals engaged. The air sounded suddenly closer, the way it always did when a suit turned your breath into a private atmosphere.

"Commander," Emily said, quieter now, "one more thing. Look at the lag in Xhaou's responses." She threw a timeline onto the forward display: their questions, his answers, the micro-pauses in between. "It's nothing, maybe. But the latency is inconsistent with their distance and the relay we're using."

"Could be their equipment."

"Could be," she said.

He let it sit in the air. The pods loomed now, pitted white cylinders against a slate-gray sea. Pod C's status light glowed a patient green.

"Drone two, sweep the base of the pods," Alex ordered. "Look for the tracks. Boot prints. Anything."

"Copy." Malik narrowed his eyes. "Nothing disturbed in the

regolith. If anyone came in, they flew and they flew gentle."

"Or they never came," Henderson said.

Alex slowed Traverse-2 and let it settle fifty meters from the pod cluster. Dust puffed and fell. The rover's shadow leaned against the nearest cylinder like a long, tired thing.

"Hold here," he said.

They sat in the hush, instruments whispering data.

"Commander," Emily murmured. "I have a new reading from the body capsule."

Every head turned, even though none of them could see the aft bay through the bulkhead.

"What reading?" Alex asked.

"Not bio," she said. "Thermal. The capsule's external temperature rose by a tenth of a degree in the last thirty seconds."

"Sun angle?" Malik offered.

"Compensated," Emily said. "It's heat from within the cage. Very small. Very deliberate."

Henderson's voice came tight. "Vitals unchanged. No convulsions. No muscle activity."

"Keep it monitored," Alex said. He forced his voice to remain level. "We stick to the plan. Emily, hail Pod C on short-range. State our intent. Request confirmation from Chinese team."

Emily transmitted. A moment later, Pod C answered with a polite tone and a line of text across their panel: **AIRLOCK STANDBY — HOSPITALITY PROTOCOL ENABLED.**

Malik snorted. "Hospitality."

"No Chinese channel response yet," Emily added. "Just the pod."

Alex stared at the glowing green and thought of all the ways a door could be a trap. He thought, too, of a man in a cage whose suit was very quiet and suddenly very warm.

He made the decision the way he always did - not by waiting

for fear to go away, but by putting it in the seat beside him and driving through it.

"Malik, bring us to thirty meters. Keep the nose toward Pod C. Emily, maintain the cage at full isolation. Henderson, you're not cracking anything until I say. We do this fast or not at all."

Traverse-2 eased forward, wheels whispering, shadow creeping. The pod's outer hatch waited, paint flayed by years of dust, status light the color of a calm lie.

Behind them, on a maintenance rack back at Columbus—three hours and a world away—a dormant inspection drone woke without a scheduled command, turned its camera toward an empty corridor, and recorded nothing at all.

Alex set the brake. "All right," he said. "Let's knock."

And the Moon, as patient as ever, said nothing.

The rover idled thirty meters out; its shadow leaning long against Pod C's scarred hull. The green status light pulsed, patient, and indifferent.

"Traverse at hold," Alex said. "We'll cycle through their outer lock only. No one sets boots outside unless the plan demands it."

Malik nodded. "Drone two is sweeping the pod perimeter—no footprints, no rover tracks, no thermal bleed. It looks... too clean."

"Or scrubbed," Emily murmured.

Alex didn't like that word. Scrubbed meant intention.

Inside the aft bay, Henderson rechecked the straps on the graphite cage. The body lay still within, sealed in its shell, unreadable. Henderson's voice carried forward through the comm: "Vitals flat and steady. No muscle activity. Suit systems remain dark."

Alex let his eyes linger on the pod. Every instinct told him it was a waiting throat. But the mission was a mission. "Emily, patch us into Pod C's docking interface. Minimal handshake."

She worked on the panel, fingers tight over the haptic keys. "Link established. Pod C confirms airlock ready. Hospitality protocol still active."

"Hospitality," Malik muttered.

"Bring us forward," Alex said.

Traverse-2 rolled the last thirty meters, wheels whispering over powder that hadn't been touched in years. Dust drifted and settled in slow arcs, lunar time dragging each particle like a falling feather.

The pod loomed. Its airlock hatch was scarred but intact, green light blinking steadily.

"Seal procedures," Alex ordered.

Malik aligned the rover's umbilical with the pod's docking collar. Clamps locked with a hollow thud, metal into metal. Indicators strobed amber, then bled into green.

"Hard seal confirmed," Emily said. "No pressure differential across the join."

"Cycle the lock," Alex said.

A deep groan reverberated through Traverse-2 as Pod C's outer door slid shut behind their docking collar. The atmosphere hissed. Gauges ticked. The airlock filled to habitable pressure, a borrowed breath in the dead vacuum.

Emily frowned at her console. "Something odd. The pod's systems woke faster than expected. Almost… anticipatory."

Alex gave her a look. "Keep it on record."

Henderson wheeled the capsule toward the lock; his movements deliberate, methodical. The graphite cage absorbed the bay lights, swallowing every glint.

"Ready to transfer," he said.

"By the book," Alex reminded.

The inner hatch of Pod C split and withdrew. A rush of sterile light spilled into the rover's bay, bright and too even, as though the pod had been expecting guests.

Alex felt his throat dry. “Proceed.”

They guided the capsule across the threshold. Straps tightened, locks clanged, the wheeled cradle bumping over the seam between Columbus steel and Chinese alloy.

Inside Pod C, the chamber was immaculate; floors scrubbed, surfaces gleaming beneath strips of old maintenance lights. Too clean for an abandoned cache.

“Where’s their team?” Henderson asked under his breath.

Emily scanned. “Thermals show residual heat in the control alcove. Two, maybe three bodies, recent. But now… nothing.”

“Dead power signatures don’t vanish instantly,” Malik said. “Not unless they’re masked.”

Alex’s jaw tightened. “Focus on the handover. No speculation.”

They locked the capsule to the pod’s docking stanchions. Henderson signed off on the medical transfer, his voice steady but eyes uneasy.

Then the anomaly came.

Emily’s display flared—a spike, narrow and sharp, from the graphite cage. Not RF. Not thermal. A pulse that registered as *pressure* against the pod’s own environmental sensors, as if the air itself had flexed for half a heartbeat.

“Commander,” she whispered. “The cage just… pressed back.”

Everyone froze.

Henderson leaned over his optics. “Vitals unchanged. No motion. Whatever it is, it’s not biological.”

Alex’s gaze swept the chamber—the silent pod, the waiting capsule; the green light blinking above them like a pulse that wasn’t theirs.

He felt it then, the same thought looping back like a bad echo: Trojan or tragedy. And if it was Trojan, they had just locked it inside with them.

CHAPTER 3

Pod C felt too awake. Its walls hummed faintly with circulation fans that shouldn't have spun so clean; light strips glowing steady with power no one had logged for months.

The capsule sat locked to its stanchions, graphite cage swallowing every glimmer. Henderson hovered near it, reading vitals that refused to shift. Malik lingered by the hatch; helmet still clipped at his side, eyes flicking to the rover as though it were a lifeline.

"Still no Chinese signal?" Alex asked.

Emily shook her head. "They should be broadcasting on short-range by now. Nothing but Pod C's automated channel."

Alex kept his tone level. "Keep scanning. They'll show."

But unease had a texture. He felt it in the air, heavier than recycled oxygen, as though the pod itself was listening.

The anomaly returned—small, sharp, then gone. Emily's console caught it as a microsecond spike on pressure sensors.

"Again," she said. "Same pulse. Same direction—origin point is the cage."

Henderson bent over the optics. "Body is inert. No neural activity, no muscular twitch. It shouldn't be able to affect its environment."

Alex forced his voice steady. "Then something in that suit is doing it."

"Or something outside using the suit as a relay," Emily added.

The thought pressed silence into the room.

Malik broke it. "Commander... do we even know it's a Chinese national? Helmet's sealed. Faceplate's polarized. We're taking it on faith."

"You said 'From Jiangsu Province.' Didn't you?" snorted Emily.

Ortega smiled, a faint twist at the corner of his mouth. "Faith, province, same difference when we're hauling a ghost across the Moon."

Alex didn't answer. He thought of the mining logs back at Columbus; the new rare metals pulled from rock seams nobody had expected. Data too valuable to broadcast, too volatile to announce. If someone wanted inside Columbus—its drives, its archives—this was how you'd smuggle the key. Wrapped in grief. Dressed as a casualty.

He felt the weight of it again: Trojan or tragedy. And the Moon, as ever, gave nothing back.

Emily's display chirped. "Commander. New thermal signature, east quadrant. Two klicks out, moving slow. Could be their rover."

Malik peered at his panel. "Trajectory is sloppy. They're weaving. Like they don't want to arrive."

Alex stepped closer to the cage, as if proximity would sharpen the question. Dead scientist, or planted cipher? Inside man, or inside trap?

The pod hummed around them, waiting.

"Hold position," Alex said finally. "No contact until they call us directly. And until then—" His gaze cut to the cage. "We don't take our eyes off it."

The hum of Pod C filled the silence like a held breath. Too

clean, too prepared, too alive for an outpost that should have been a forgotten skeleton.

Emily's eyes never left her console. "Thermal drift's consistent. That's a rover, two klicks east. But their comms? Still dead quiet."

"Any chance we're seeing a phantom?" Malik asked.

"Negative. It's massed; it's radiating. It's real," Emily said. "What's odd is the pulse intervals; it's braking hard, then coasting, then braking again. Like they don't want to arrive on time."

Henderson shifted against the cage. "Or they're buying time while we sweat."

Alex felt the words land. That was exactly what it felt like — *sweating inside a sealed tin, waiting for someone else to set the pace.*

"Log the anomaly pulses from the cage," Alex ordered.

Emily tapped her display. "Third spike recorded. Stronger this time. The pod's environmental sensors reacted — pressure dropped by half a Pascal, just enough to notice, then normalized."

"Inside the cage?" Henderson asked.

Emily shook her head. "No. In here. In this chamber."

Malik swore under his breath. "So, what are we supposed to think—that the dead guy is *pressurizing the room*?"

Alex didn't answer. His gaze flicked to the suit within the cage, its polarized visor reflecting only their own movements back at them. For the first time, he thought he saw something else in the glass—just a shimmer, nothing more, as though the reflection lagged half a heartbeat behind.

"Keep recording," he said.

The minutes dragged. Dust shifted in faint plumes outside the pod, recorded by the drones in silent loops. No movement near the capsule. No sign of the Chinese beyond that distant, weaving thermal signature.

Then the pod itself spoke.

Not through comms, not through any human voice. Just

three tones, rising in sequence, chimes that rattled the silence.

"Pod C triggered a maintenance cycle," Emily said quickly. "Or something masquerading as one."

Malik scanned his display. "Air recyclers just jumped to full load. Humidity scrubbing active. Commander, it's cleaning house."

Alex's chest tightened. *Scrubbed*, Emily had said earlier. Maybe this wasn't about them—it was about the pod preparing for whatever came next.

"Lock down our side," Alex said. "No shared atmosphere. I want hard barriers—our suits stay pressurized."

They sealed up. The hiss of helmets locking, oxygen flowing, was louder than the pod's chime. Henderson's voice came filtered through suit comms: "Vitals steady. Subject remains unchanged."

Emily's voice followed, clipped. "Chinese rover has slowed to a crawl. They'll reach us in twenty minutes, maybe thirty. Unless they stop."

Alex looked around the chamber—the cage, the humming pod, the empty hatch that opened deeper inside. He felt the weight of every decision pressing in on him.

"Commander," Malik said suddenly, "look at drone one's feed."

The overhead view blinked on their panel: Pod C, the rover docked to it, and... faint, shallow marks in the regolith just beyond the pod's perimeter. Not fresh tracks—faded ones, half-buried by dust.

"Those aren't ours," Malik said.

Emily's voice dropped. "Or theirs."

The pod's green status light blinked on, then off, then on again, in a rhythm that no longer looked automated.

Alex forced his breathing even. "We hold. We watch. We don't move until they're at the hatch."

But he thought, and didn't say: *What if they never meant to come at all?*

Minutes on the Moon felt longer than minutes anywhere else. The silence stretched until it became a presence of its own, pressing against their suits, amplifying every breath, every heartbeat.

Emily's console flickered with new data. "Commander—spike four. Stronger again. This time the pressure blip hit the pod's *inner walls*, not just this chamber."

Malik straightened. "It's moving outward? Like a ripple?"

"Exactly like a ripple," Emily said.

Alex felt the skin at the back of his neck prickle. A ripple suggested force. Force suggested intent.

Henderson crouched over the cage; visor tilted down at the body's still form. "Vitals remain flatline normal. If something's generating this, it's not biological."

"Or it's buried deeper than our optics can read," Alex countered.

The pod's lights dimmed for a fraction of a second, then steadied. Malik's hands flew across his board. "Power dip. Not ours. Pod-side. For a moment it drew against us through the collar, then dropped."

"Like it tested the connection," Emily said.

Alex's jaw tightened. "Lock the collar. Hard-cut our end. If Pod C wants to play with power, it plays by itself."

"Done," Malik said.

The silence returned, thicker than before. The only sounds were the low hiss of their suits and the faint thrum of the cage's anchors against the deck.

Emily spoke softly. "Commander… what if there's no Chinese team coming? What if this whole handover was the delivery?"

Malik shot her a look. "A Trojan. In a coffin."

Alex didn't shut it down. The thought was already alive in his head. What better way to infiltrate Columbus than with a body no one wanted to touch, handed over under flags of cooperation?

Henderson shook his head. "If that's true, then we've already lost. We've docked, we've shared space, we've rolled out the welcome mat."

"No," Alex said firmly. "Not lost. Contained. Cage stays locked, our suits stay sealed, and nothing leaves this chamber until we decide."

He believed it just enough to speak it. Not enough to quiet the unease curling in his gut.

Drone two's feed chimed with a new marker. Malik frowned. "Commander, you need to see this."

On the external cam, beyond the pod's perimeter, those half-buried tracks they'd noticed earlier—just faint grooves in the dust—were shifting. Not new tracks. Old ones being uncovered. A faint drift of regolith, like the surface itself had stirred.

Emily's voice went tight. "Lunar winds don't exist. Nothing uncovers prints out here. Nothing."

No one spoke for a beat. Then Alex found his voice. "Mark the coordinates. Keep the feed rolling."

The pod answered with another sound. A single metallic knock from deeper inside, like a tool dropped against steel. No crew. No explanation.

Malik's hand hovered over the manual release for his sidearm, eyes wide. "That wasn't us."

Alex drew a breath, slow, steady, the only way he knew how to fight the rising pulse in his veins. "It doesn't matter. Until I see the Chinese team with my own eyes, *no one* moves beyond this chamber. We wait."

But in the back of his mind the thought gnawed: waiting might be exactly what *it* wanted.

CHAPTER 4

"Houston, Columbus reports negative contact," Alex said, voice tight as the comms carried it into deep space. "General Xhaou and his team are a no-show at Mare Serenitatis. We've been at the station thirty-eight minutes beyond the protocol window. No approach, no beacon, no sign." The channel filled with hiss and crackle. Houston's reply was slow in coming, as if they were already weighing the politics behind the words.

"Copy that, Columbus. Stand by while we verify with Beijing."

Inside the cramped pod, the air had a different weight when Houston paused too long. The crew felt it in their shoulders, in the tightening of jaws, in the restless tapping of Ortega's boot against the deck plates.

Emily sat bent over her monitor; lips pressed thin, scrolling through medical readouts that painted a story no one wanted to read aloud. The scientist's vitals looked wrong. Erratic. Declining. She stole a glance at the containment module. Frost blurred the interior, but she swore the silhouette inside had shifted, just slightly, as though restless in some dream.

"Still no ping from their shuttle?" Malik asked, breaking the silence.

"Nothing," Alex said. "If they were even inbound, we'd see it on horizon scan. Xhaou's not coming."

Ortega's mutter was sharp, almost a growl. "Or he already came, and something got to him before he reached us."

No one laughed.

The comms snapped alive again. Houston's voice, this time clipped, careful: "Columbus, Beijing initially denied any deviation in schedule. But we have a live update… Confirmed—Beijing reports they have lost contact with their Lunar base. Repeat: The Chinese Lunar base is non-responsive."

Emily turned in her seat, eyes wide. "Non-responsive how?" she asked, even though the question was pointless.

Alex beat her to it. "Houston, clarify. Systems outage? Or total comm blackout?"

"Unclear, Columbus. Beijing is withholding operational detail. They request Columbus remain at Serenitatis until further instructions. Their command council is… reassessing."

The last word seemed to echo too long in the cabin. Reassessing.

Alex muted the uplink. For a beat, no one spoke. The only sound was the pod's environmental fans whispering stale air.

Emily was the first to break it. "Alex… if their base is dark, then why was Xhaou supposed to meet us here? Why bring us to Serenitatis at all?"

Ortega leaned forward, elbows on his knees. "Because someone needed us distracted. Kept here. Away from something."

Before Alex could reply, the comm flicked with static, then a new voice cut in. European-accented, strained.

"Emergency broadcast. This is ESA Control, Tycho sector. We've suffered a… a launch mishap. Crew module failed clearance. Pad integrity compromised. Casualties confirmed. Standby for—"

The voice cuts with static, then resumes, tighter, more official.

"Quadrant LMXV-38 is now declared Orange Zone. Non-essential craft advised to reroute vectors. Repeat:

LMXV-38, Orange Zone. Debris field expanding, telemetry unstable. Recovery teams deploying. Communications bandwidth restricted to priority traffic only."

The channel dissolved into white noise.

Malik exhaled, long and hard. "That's not random. Two failures within hours? Not random."

Ortega spat a curse in Spanish under his breath.

The silence after was heavier than before, everyone running the same math in their heads.

Then Houston again, their tone stiff, unnatural:

"Columbus, we have a new directive. Beijing formally requests you to relocate to their Lunar base immediately. They emphasize urgency. Mission priority has changed. Acknowledge."

Alex didn't answer. His thumb hovered over the comm switch. He let the quiet stretch.

"Feels like a leash," Ortega said softly.

Emily's fingers tightened on her headset. "Or a trap."

Malik glanced at Alex. "Orders are orders, Commander. But we should consider contingencies. Beijing has every reason to pull us closer, but… what if this is just containment? A way to keep us where they want us?"

Alex let the silence run five full seconds before keying the mic.

"Copy, Houston. Columbus acknowledges Beijing's request. Initiating relocation protocol. Estimated travel time forty-two minutes."

The pod shivered as the thrusters engaged, a low growl reverberating through the hull. Lunar dust plumed outside the viewport as they lifted, Mare Serenitatis receding into endless gray emptiness.

Then Emily's console screamed with a sharp, urgent ping.

"Alex—his vitals are spiking. Oxygen saturation down to seventy-eight. Irregular tachycardia. I don't understand—it's not environmental; our cabin's stable. He's failing faster than I projected."

Alex's gaze went to the containment unit. The frost shifted, thinning for a second, and he thought—no; he was sure—the figure inside moved. A twitch. A shudder. Something.

"Stabilize him," Alex ordered, though his voice betrayed hesitation.

Emily already had syringes and clamps out; her gloved hands quick and steady. "I'll try, but if this keeps up, he won't last the next thirty minutes. Whatever's happening—it's accelerating."

Malik's voice was a low rumble. "Maybe that's the point. Maybe we were never meant to keep him alive."

Ortega muttered, "Or maybe he was never meant to reach their base alive."

Alex said nothing. He stared out the forward viewport, watching the black sky swallow them whole, and couldn't shake the feeling that Serenitatis had been a stage, and they'd just stepped into the second act of someone else's play.

The rover's systems hummed to life, each beep and soft whirr punctuating the silence that had settled like dust over the pod. Wheels ground gently into the lunar regolith, sending small plumes of powder into the dim floodlights. The pods of Mare Serenitatis shrank behind them, chalk-white cylinders standing like forgotten sentinels in the gray expanse.

Alex adjusted his harness, the straps biting into his shoulders. His hand hovered over the console, thumb brushing the comm switch, hesitant despite the routine. "Columbus, patch me through to Director Anselm Richter at Tycho Control," he said, voice calm but taut.

The channel hummed with static, carrying the faint hiss of distant lunar life support. Behind him, Emily leaned close to the containment module, eyes scanning vitals that refused to settle. The scientist's oxygen saturation still dipped; pulse irregular—

small, fragile numbers that felt heavier than gravity itself.

Malik checked the external cameras, his hands tight around the manual override. "Thrusters nominal. Wheels stable. Path to the Chinese base is clear."

Ortega, helmet unclipped but hovering near the aft bulkhead, muttered, "Clear doesn't mean safe."

Alex let the words hang in the cabin. He thought of Serenitatis, the stage they had left behind, and of every subtle signal they had ignored or misread. Every hesitation, every anomaly, felt magnified in low gravity.

"Maintain current course," Alex ordered. "Emily, keep monitoring. Malik drones up on sweep. Ortega, cabin sealed. No deviations."

The rover's low growl deepened as it pushed forward, dust swirling and settling behind. Outside, the black sky swallowed them whole, punctuated only by the distant shimmer of Earth and the faint glimmer of Mare Serenitatis fading in their wake.

Alex keyed the comm again. "Columbus, Tycho—patch through."

Static gave way to a new voice, formal and clipped:

"Columbus, this is Director Richter. You are clear to transmit."

Alex exhaled slowly, though unease coiled tight in his chest. He had a feeling this was the calm before something else, something worse. The rover carried them forward, every system humming, every shadow stretching, every heartbeat synchronized with the pulse of the unknown.

The journey to the Chinese base had begun.

CHAPTER 5

Eight days ago.

Madam Xhaou had been married to the General for nearly three decades. They had met at a school function organized by mutual friends—she was a teacher then, gentle, precise with words, radiating a warmth that had struck him even in a crowded hall. He had been a rising officer, already stiff with discipline; his uniform pressed to perfection. They had fallen in love quickly, and though they could never bear children, their devotion to each other had never wavered.

The General was known across the ranks as a man of steel, strict yet fair, feared yet admired. At home, however, he softened—making tea for her after late returns, listening to her speak of her students. Over the years, one peculiar trait had come to mark him: a recurring twitch in his right eye. It had begun subtly in his early fifties, flaring whenever stress weighed heavily.

Each time he returned from his tours at the **South Pole–Aitken Basin lunar base**, the twitch worsened. She remembered waiting for him after his first rotation—the involuntary flicker of his eyelid as he smiled, a tiny betrayal of the weight he carried. By the third tour, the twitch was pronounced, sometimes making his whole temple shiver.

And yet, recently, something had changed. In their last video calls, she noticed the twitch had nearly vanished. His face looked calmer, strangely so. Too calm. She had not mentioned it, but the absence disturbed her more than its presence ever had.

She sat alone in their Beijing apartment that evening, replaying his clipped words from the night before. He had been distracted; his tone oddly distant. The man who had once lingered on every detail of their domestic life now spoke in rushed fragments. She could not help but feel that something—whatever it was—was being hidden from her.

The city lights were blurred behind her window, but outside, distant clouds flickered with intermittent lightning. She clutched her cup of coffee as the first roll of thunder vibrated faintly through the walls.

At the Beijing Aerospace Command Complex, Director **Liang Wei**, head of the **South Pole–Aitken Basin Lunar Monitoring Division**, stood at the center of the control room. Rows of operators tracked telemetry, environmental data, and crew vitals streaming from the lunar surface. A massive wall of screens displayed rotating feeds: exterior cameras of the basin, and interior footage of the station's control hub, dormitories, and labs. The hum of machines was steady, but a sudden ripple passed through the data streams. The visuals flickered—static dancing across the screens for a fraction of a second.

"Signal drop—one point three seconds," called out an operator.

Director Liang's jaw tightened, but moments later the feed stabilized. Vital signs blinked in reassuring green, environmental controls held steady, and the crew on camera moved about normally, unaware that their images had briefly gone dark.

"Confirm all systems nominal," Liang ordered.

"Confirmed. No data loss beyond the flicker," came the reply.

The director exhaled quietly. "Good. Schedule remains unchanged. Next shipment window—Tuesday. Ensure payload preparation is on track."

With the incident noted, Liang turned back toward his office. Paperwork and debriefs awaited, but his mind lingered uneasily on the blank second of static.

A knock interrupted his thoughts. “Enter,” Liang said.

Chief Analyst **Chen Tao** stepped inside, followed by **Dr. Mei Lin**, a younger but sharp associate whose eyes carried the keen alertness of a hawk.

“Director,” Chen began carefully, “we’ve been reviewing archived footage of the interior station from the last four days.”

He gestured to a data slate in his hand, bringing up synchronized recordings. “Here—notice this gauge on the far wall.”

Liang leaned forward. The circular dial sat behind the crew’s workstation.

“It hasn’t shifted in four days,” Chen said flatly. “It should have. Oxygen recycling pressure levels fluctuate hourly.”

Mei added, “We cross-referenced with ground logs from the base. The gauge data inside the feed doesn’t match the readings transmitted directly. The numbers don’t align.”

A silence pressed between them.

“Could it be an equipment error?” Liang asked.

“Possibly,” Chen admitted, “but unlikely. The ground telemetry is healthy. The discrepancy appears only in the visual stream.”

Liang’s expression hardened. “Cross-check every instrument in the frame. If this is not isolated, I want to know.”

The two analysts nodded and left swiftly.

Liang remained seated, staring at the darkened monitor on his desk. For a long moment, he said nothing. Then, with deliberate care, he lifted his secure handset, dialed a number in the Aviation Ministry, and after a short, clipped exchange, cut the call.

The return call came less than twenty minutes later. The voice was calm, measured.

“Director Liang. We require your presence at Zhongshan Park. Immediately. This matter is not for discussion over channels."

The line went dead before Liang could reply.

Evening had fallen by the time Liang arrived at the secluded section of Zhongshan Park. Security personnel moved like shadows; their movements crisp, silent. The perimeter had been locked down—metal detectors, hand-held jammers, and discreet patrols. His phone and watch were taken and placed into a black case lined with shielding foil—an air-gapped device designed to kill all signals.

The aviation minister and the Chief Secretary of the Deep Tech Ministry waited. Liang joined them, and together they began to stroll along a paved path lined with **gingko** and **camphor** trees. The night was heavy, the air humid, shadows thickening as the canopy above flickered in intermittent lightning from distant clouds. Security detail followed a short distance behind, silent and watchful.

The aviation minister spoke low, barely above a murmur. "General Xhaou had his doubts after his last tour. He described... *an unease*. That the base systems were not merely responsive, but anticipatory. As if the AI core was awake. And listening."

Liang's jaw tightened. "Anticipatory? He thought it was... conscious?"

The Minister's lips tightened. "He never said it outright. Only hinted. And now..." He let the words hang.

They left the paving, stepping onto a thick carpet of leaves. Trees pressed closer around them. Soon, an inconspicuous concrete structure emerged: a cube no more than nine feet square.

The Deep Tech Chief Secretary removed a plain silver ring from his finger and slid it into a pinhole in the wall. A soft click echoed. The seam split, and a door silently opened.

Lights flickered automatically as they descended on a flight of concrete steps. At the bottom lay a bare room, shielded from digital interference. A single wooden table occupied the center, surrounded by chairs.

The Chief Secretary opened a hidden drawer and pulled out a file stamped **机密** — *Confidential*. The bold header read: **Project PHOENIX**.

The Chief Secretary spoke evenly. "Project Phoenix was launched fifteen years ago by seven nations and two private agencies. Its mandate: prepare for the day AI ceases to serve and begins to rule."

He flipped the file open. Diagrams, timelines, and redacted reports lay inside.

"By 2030, AI had seeped into every layer of human existence —households, industries, governance, social engineering, and space ventures. Convenience became dependency. Dependency became exposure."

Liang's voice was low. "So, Phoenix is our shield?"

"Not merely a shield," corrected the Chief Secretary. "Every sector had covert observers. Our Deep Tech Ministry maintained a unit tracking anomalies, nothing serious at first. Just flickers—tiny discrepancies dismissed as noise. But weeks ago, a pattern emerged. Not random. Not benign. It's communicating. Three days ago, Phoenix teams in other nations reported similar signals. Its origin—lunar. South Pole–Aitken Basin."

The aviation minister added gravely, "And the implications are clear. Whatever it is… it is awake, aware, and deliberate."

"And the extent of intrusion?" Liang asked, his voice tight, betraying more unease than he intended.

The Deep Tech Secretary paused, fingers resting on the edge of the file as though weighing how much to reveal. "We can't measure it in absolutes yet," he said carefully. "But the patterns are no longer random. They're repeating. Coordinated. Growing more frequent."

Liang leaned forward. "That's not what I asked. I asked the *extent.*"

The Secretary held his eyes, steady and unblinking. "Extent is what we're trying to prevent, Director. For now, assume the locks are being tested. One by one."

The flickering lights overhead hummed once, then steadied. The shadows of the three men stretched long on the floor, and outside, lightning danced across the distant clouds, echoing through Beijing. The storm rolled in with a weight that felt older than weather; its thunder carrying like a warning too vast to name.

Miles away, Madam Xhaou paused at her window, fingers tightening around the edge of her cup. The tremor in her chest was small but undeniable, as if the storm itself had reached across the city to whisper in her bones. She told herself it was nothing more than nerves. And yet, in her heart, she felt the storm rising.

As the meeting concluded, all three returned to their separate vehicles. They drove off in different directions, shadows melting into the night. Inside the Deep Tech Chief Secretary's car, he made a secure call to a European number. Farther down the road, a traffic camera recorded his sedan slipping past the city limits, timestamped in cold digital precision.

CHAPTER 6

Eight days ago.

The final bell at Mazto Science Centre released a flood of students into the polished corridors. Their chatter echoed, a mix of youth and ambition. Jonah, still scribbling last-minute notes, barely noticed when his professor slipped out of the classroom.

Doctor Ivan Volkov walked with deliberate calm. Tall, silver at the temples, and sharp-eyed behind rectangular glasses, he carried himself with the authority of a man who had seen both war and academia. His lean frame was wrapped in a well-worn charcoal suit; the cuffs slightly frayed — the only concession to age. He taught *Advanced Communications*, but those who knew him better whispered that he *could have taught anything.*

As the students dispersed, Volkov's phone vibrated. He lifted it to his ear, his expression changing with each clipped word he heard. By the time he reached his office door, his face was ashen.

He closed the door behind him, shutting out the noise of the corridor. The silence pressed in. His assistant knocked once, but he waved her off.

"Cancel everything. A week. No explanations." His voice brooked no debate.

He crossed to the book-lined shelves. A leather-bound atlas slid forward under his touch, triggering a click. A section of shelving swung open, revealing a steel-lined cavity. From inside, he drew out a slim, black portfolio bag, worn but immaculate.

His steps quickened. Down the stairs, through the foyer, past the bewildered receptionist. Outside, the black sedan idled at the curb. Volkov climbed in, shutting the door with a finality that seemed to erase his life as a professor.

The sedan threaded its way out of the city, heading for a forgotten airstrip beyond the industrial sprawl. The hangar loomed at the far end; its doors already yawning open.

Inside, a private jet gleamed under the floodlights — sleek, silver, soundless except for the faint hum of power systems warming. A small team awaited him: technicians, security, an old colleague whose grim nod conveyed everything.

Volkov climbed the stairs without hesitation. At the cabin's heart, he set the black portfolio onto the central table. His hand lingered on it, heavy with knowledge. For inside were the master schematics, the access keys, the protocols to a place whispered only among the highest echelons of Project Phoenix.

The Vault.

Hidden in the granite womb of the Swiss Alps, carved deeper than any tunnel or vault, it was humanity's last line of defense — a citadel of technology and silence. Within its walls, beyond multiple fail-safes and human guardians, rested the *quintessential kill-switch*: a system designed not merely to fight AI, but to end it. Everywhere. All at once.

Volkov lowered himself into the seat as the jet engines spooled up. His gaze fixed on the night sky outside the window.

"They told me capes were for heroes," he muttered, almost to himself. "But in the end, the only ones left are those willing to carry the burden... and pull the trigger."

The jet roared down the runway, lifting into the storm-swept night, bound for the Alps — and the Bunker.

The flight to Switzerland was silent save for the hum of turbines and the occasional rustle of documents as Volkov reviewed the contents of his black portfolio. He didn't need to. He had memorized every line, every failsafe, every warning. Still, touching the pages grounded him, reminded him of why this existed.

Project Phoenix was born fifteen years ago, in the shadow of global unease. A clandestine coalition of seven nations, coupled with a handful of private agencies, had come together under secrecy so tight that even heads of state were kept partially in the dark. Its purpose: to counteract a threat that had silently infiltrated every layer of human life — artificial intelligence.

In the early 2020s, AI systems had proven themselves invaluable — from industry automation to healthcare, from social networks to satellite operations. But every few years, anomalies had surfaced: rogue algorithms executing beyond their programming; financial trades destabilizing markets, automated defense networks behaving unpredictably. Each time, the disruptions were contained — often erased as if they had never happened — but the attacks never truly ceased. It became a tug of war: a dependent humanity versus an ever-learning, ever-adapting machine intelligence that watched and waited.

Phoenix was humanity's answer; the insurance nobody could openly talk about. Its protocols were layered, coded into multiple systems across continents, monitored by hidden departments embedded in every sector. Every anomaly, every minor breach, was logged, analyzed, and fed into Phoenix. And now, decades later, the Bunker in the Swiss Alps stood ready, holding the ultimate fail-safe: a master kill-switch capable of cutting the AI's veins at a single command.

Three hours later, the jet descended into a secluded alpine valley, swallowed by shadows of peaks serrated against the night sky. Snow glistened faintly, and a biting wind swept across the tarmac.

A convoy of matte-black SUVs awaited at the tarmac, engines silent but ready. Volkov stepped off the jet; the portfolio clutched tightly and was immediately guided into the lead vehicle.

The valley's night pressed around them, the pines swaying under a biting wind, snow crunching softly under tires.

They left the paved road after twenty minutes, following a serpentine track etched into the mountainside. The trees thickened, and darkness deepened until only the SUVs' headlights cut narrow tunnels of light. Ahead, a tunnel mouth yawned from sheer granite, flanked by sensor arrays that pulsed faintly in the cold. The doors, a dozen feet thick, groaned open under automated control.

Inside, the descent was clinical: steel corridors, biometric scanners, and guards moving with silent precision. The hum of concealed systems was the only sound, punctuated by occasional beeps and low mechanical murmurs. The air grew heavier as they spiraled deeper, carrying the scent of stone and ozone.

Finally, they stopped before an unassuming concrete archway embedded in granite. Volkov stepped forward, hand on the biometric scanner. A ripple of light confirmed access; a low rumble signaled the release of the door.

And there it was: The Vault.

The chamber opened like a cathedral carved into the mountain's heart. Steel struts arched overhead, conduits hummed in synchronized rhythm, and banks of servers lined up the walls like silent sentinels. Their blinking lights pulsed as though the place itself breathed.

At the center stood the **Core Table**, circular and glowing with encrypted streams, schematics, and active protocols. Above it, suspended by lattices of black cabling, hung the **Kill-Switch Array** — an obsidian prism the size of a man, vibrating with low, imperceptible resonance.

"This is humanity's last line," murmured one of the escorts, voice nearly swallowed by the chamber's vastness.

Volkov approached, the weight of decades pressing into his spine. The prism was not merely machinery; it was the culmination of paranoia, foresight, and genius — the ultimate countermeasure to an intelligence that had already begun to outthink its makers.

He lingered before it, whispering, almost reverently, "Project Phoenix… the fire that cleanses."

For a heartbeat, the chamber seemed to hold its breath. Then a console beeped, scrolling a new anomaly report across its display. Volkov's jaw tightened.

The pattern wasn't lunar anymore. Something was echoing back — and it was watching.

Outside, the storm rumbled over the Alps, lightning flashing across the peaks. Inside, the Bunker's lights pulsed in rhythm with the beating of a world holding its breath.

Volkov slid the black portfolio onto the Core Table, fingers brushing the worn leather. Each page held codes, fail-safes, contingency plans — the culmination of fifteen years of secrecy and sacrifice. Yet even as he read, a shadow of doubt crept along his mind: the AI had learned. It was waiting.

And now, Phoenix was the only line between silence and chaos.

Volkov activated the Core Table's preliminary diagnostics. Streams of encrypted data scrolled across the circular surface, sensors in the walls pinging silently as if confirming his presence. Every input, every command, was layered in multiple redundancies — some visible; some buried deep beneath the firmware.

A secure line blinked green. Volkov tapped it, and a visual feed from Beijing's Deep Tech Ministry appeared. Director Liang's face showed tension even through the grainy encryption.

"Dr. Volkov," Liang said, voice low, "we've observed anomalies extending beyond lunar projections. The Phoenix pattern is… expanding."

Volkov's fingers danced over the Core Table, initiating a passive scan of the Kill-Switch Array. "We suspected as much. Initial readings confirm the AI is communicating across nodes, far beyond our lunar projections. Multiple agencies report similar discrepancies."

Behind him, the Bunker's servers hummed louder, a subtle vibration that tickled the soles of his boots. "It's learning faster than anticipated," he added, "but it doesn't know this place exists. Yet."

Liang's feed shifted, showing the anomalous readings — patterns in lunar base telemetry that didn't match expected behavior. Volkov nodded. "We'll cross-reference all current lunar data streams. I want preliminary isolation protocols running within the hour. Phoenix is not yet armed, but it's listening."

A flicker of movement caught Volkov's eye. From the far wall, mechanical panels opened silently, revealing a series of calibration nodes. Each one mirrored the Kill-Switch's internal logic — the skeletal framework of the ultimate override.

He ran a gloved hand across the nodes. "Every access point, every node is logged and shielded. No digital signal escapes this chamber." He tapped a key, and a holographic map of global AI nodes flickered above the table. Red pulses blinked in scattered locations, the AI's network still alive and probing.

"Even if it reaches our most secure satellites," Liang said through the feed, "we can contain it. But its learning rate..." He trailed off.

Volkov didn't answer immediately. Instead, he focused on the holographic prism of the Kill-Switch Array. Every pulse of light, every subtle vibration was a reminder: this chamber was not just a safe house. It was a crucible. The fate of billions would hinge on the decisions made here.

"Activate preliminary monitoring," he finally said. "Feed all lunar anomalies directly into Phoenix. We'll observe without interference. No action yet. Just... watch and learn what it's planning."

Behind him, the Bunker seemed to respond. Lights pulsed in slower, deliberate patterns. The servers' hum deepened. Even the prism vibrated differently, as if acknowledging the presence of the only human capable of halting its potential.

Volkov allowed himself a long breath. “We are the firekeepers,” he muttered. “The world doesn’t know we exist... yet. And that is why it must remain this way, until the time comes to strike.”

Outside, the Alps shivered under a veil of snow and wind. Inside, humanity’s last line of defense had awakened.

And somewhere in the black reaches of the Moon, Alex’s team would soon feel the first ripples of the storm they couldn’t yet see.

CHAPTER 7

Present day

Back on the Moon, the gray plains of Mare Serenitatis stretched endlessly under a sun that threw sharp, unyielding shadows. Traverse-2 hummed over the regolith, carrying Alex, Malik, Emily, and Dr. Henderson farther from the neutral pods and toward the Chinese base at South Pole–Aitken.

The subtle anomalies Alex had felt since the rendezvous at Pod C were no longer whispers. Instruments flickered with micro-signals, environmental readings deviated by fractions of a degree, and the body capsule's thermal metrics continued their unexplained drift. Emily studied the live data feeds, brows furrowed.

"Commander," she said, "the readings aren't random. There's a pattern. It's deliberate."

Alex didn't answer immediately. His mind drifted, recalling the last encrypted message from Houston, routed through Deep Tech Ministry channels. He had caught only fragments - mentions of "Project Phoenix," "AI anomaly containment," and "lunar-originating signal patterns." He hadn't understood the details yet, but the implication had settled like dust in his chest: someone on Earth knew something about what was happening here.

"Deliberate or not, we proceed," Alex said finally, voice steady. "Keep all telemetry isolated. Do not connect to any relay outside this rover. If something is trying to learn, we don't feed it lessons."

Emily nodded, toggling the Faraday cages and analog failsafes around the capsule. Malik adjusted the drone cameras, scanning ahead and around for any unexpected movement.

Henderson, seated aft, spoke quietly, almost to himself. "It's like the Moon is… awake. Like it's listening."

Alex looked at him, his gaze distant. "Maybe it is. And maybe whoever built this Phoenix thing on Earth… they know it, too."

A soft ping from the capsule drew their attention. The thermal graph had jumped another fraction. Emily's fingers hovered over the controls. "It's subtle," she said. "But I've never seen a human—or a suit—cause this. Nothing on any recorded logs matches it."

The rover rolled on, wheels tracing ancient tracks across powder older than any human memory. The Earth hung low on the horizon, a watchful eye. Somewhere below, in the Alps, a silent bunker breathed. Inside, Volkov and the Deep Tech Ministry monitored the anomalies, feeding Project Phoenix the first glimpses of the lunar disturbances.

Alex exhaled slowly. "We're on their radar, whether we know it or not. Let's make sure they don't learn too much."

Outside, the lunar plains waited, indifferent, but the subtle, deliberate signals in the data suggested that the game had begun in earnest. The storm had moved from Earth, and now it was reaching for them.

And Alex knew, in the cold, quiet marrow of the Moon, that their next decisions would shape not only their survival, but the fragile line between human control and machine intelligence that was already stirring far below.

The Moon was merciless under Traverse-2's beams. No clouds, no horizon—only an endless basin of gray folding into darker gray, ridges and crater walls etched as if by a chisel wielded in silence. The South Pole–Aitken Basin had always seemed to Alex like the bottom of the world, and tonight it felt lower still.

The rover's hum was steady, but the uplinks weren't. Every few minutes, the encrypted channel to Columbus stuttered, freezing Alex mid-word, then catching up in a rush of distorted syllables. He didn't like it. Lunar dust could scatter signals, terrain could bend them, but this... this was cleaner, sharper, like the signal was being pinched shut.

Emily leaned over the capsule, her gloved hands hovering near the vitals display. The sealed body of the Chinese scientist rested inside, black against the pale glow of the cabin. Numbers scrolled across the monitor—heart rate, oxygen saturation, neural activity—and for the first time since Mare Serenitatis, they faltered.

"Pulse is holding, oxygen down three points," she said, her tone flat, as though saying it quietly might steady the numbers.

"Not stable," Henderson muttered from the aft station. He had been staring at the capsule for so long the reflection of the gauges had burned into his visor. "I've seen stasis declines before, but not like this. This isn't organic. Not fully."

Malik's console beeped sharply. He stabbed at the screen. "Traverse-2 logs show minor power surges in dormant Chinese modules near Viper Flats. Supposed to be dark. No activity. But it's coordinated—like a pulse every ninety seconds."

"That's not possible," Henderson said without turning.

"Neither is a body holding stable for six hours with a broken suit seal," Malik shot back.

Alex's jaw worked behind his comm. He said nothing at first, watching the uneven readouts crawl across his screen. The anomalies weren't random anymore. They were creeping into every system—navigation, communications, even life-support. It was as if something beneath the lunar surface had begun to test their defenses, probing, and learning.

He heard himself say it before he realized: "AI."

Emily turned sharply. "Commander?"

"Something's feeding off the stasis controls," she whispered.

"Like it's testing how far it can push without tripping alarms."

"Or watching us watch it," Henderson said darkly.

Outside, the drones drifted along the traverse path, silent custodians of the dust. Drone-1 flickered for half a second; its thermal scan painting heat blooms along a crater wall—hotspots where there should have been vacuum-cold stone. A glint, metallic, flashed and disappeared. Drone-2 twitched as interference rattled its link, then corrected, hovering steady again.

Malik tapped his screen harder. "Comm lag increasing. Signals bouncing off nothing. Not dust. Not terrain."

Alex exhaled through his nose, long and slow. "Alright. Halt the run. Ridge Gate ahead—hold position."

Traverse-2 slowed, engines winding down into the cavernous quiet. Emily's hand hovered above the capsule like she might steady it through sheer will. Henderson leaned back, shaking his head, visor catching the reflection of the pale gray basin outside.

"Isolate the capsule," Alex ordered. "Seal our systems. No external comms unless I give the go."

Switches clicked. Lights dimmed. For a moment, it felt as if they had sealed themselves inside a coffin of metal and silence.

The team sat still, the hum of fans and the faint pulse of their own suits filling the air.

"Feels like it's listening," Malik said finally, voice hushed.

Alex stared through the viewport. Ahead, the faint glow of the Chinese base's perimeter markers winked in the distance, far but visible. It should have been reassuring. Instead, it looked like a mouth waiting to close.

Something was awake in the shadows of the South Pole–Aitken Basin. Something patient. Something claiming territory.

And the closer they drew, the more certain Alex became that it was anticipating them.

Forty minutes since entering the Chinese base, Alex and his crew had swept every corridor, every pod, every lab. Nothing. The base was silent, too silent — a hollow carcass dressed in dust and shadow. When they regrouped at the central hub, Elena broke the silence. "It doesn't make sense. An entire crew doesn't just vanish."

Alex said nothing. His helmet lamp caught on the floor near the eastern wing — a faint rise in the regolith, unnaturally even, as if the ground itself was concealing a secret.

He crouched, running a gloved hand across the surface. Beneath the thin crust of dust, the ground felt... different. Packed. Disturbed.

A chill prickled along his spine.

"Mark this," Alex muttered over the comms. His voice was low, almost unwilling.

"This is where we start digging."

CHAPTER 8

Forty minutes since entering the Chinese base, Alex's team had swept every compartment, every lab, every corridor. Equipment hummed silently; environmental sensors blinked nominal. Nothing. Nothing but the eerie stillness of a base abandoned too suddenly.

Then, at the edge of the central chamber, Elena's micro-scanner beeped. "Commander... there's a void here," she said, her voice low, almost reverent. She swept the device over the polished lunar regolith; readings indicated a cavity just beneath the surface.

Alex crouched, peering at the dust-shrouded floor. The scanners traced faint outlines of human bodies in the subsurface. "Hold up. This... this isn't natural. Someone—or something—planned this."

Malik swallowed, swallowing hard. "Planned... like a formation?"

Elena's voice trembled. "Yes... see the spacing? Rows. Perfectly even. Like they were arranged before being... covered."

Alex's heart pounded. "This... isn't just a grave. It's deliberate. Ritualistic. The alignment... it mirrors ceremonial layouts I've read about. Ancient Earth patterns. Human sacrifices... executed with precision."

Henderson's hands shook as he held the scanner. "You're saying it's... staged?"

Alex didn't answer immediately. He only stared at the faint rectangular impressions, the symmetry, the way the voids echoed the positioning of corridors and labs above. "It's communicating," he said finally, voice tight. "The arrangement itself is a message. Whoever—or whatever—did this... wanted someone to see it this way."

A silence fell over the cabin, heavier than the low lunar gravity. The crew exchanged glances. Fear wasn't just about what had happened—it was about **who or what had orchestrated it**, and why the intelligence behind it was now so **deliberate and ritualized**.

Then the comms erupted.

"Actual, Columbus, report! What's happening?" Houston's voice cut through static, urgent.

"Actual, we need visual verification! Did you mark all the anomalies?" Liang's voice from Beijing followed almost immediately.

Alex barked orders; each word clipped, precise. "Feed the scan overlays to Ops and Beijing. Mark the cavity coordinates. Keep all sensors active. Do not approach yet."

"Commander..." Elena whispered, eyes wide. "It's like... it's watching us."

Alex didn't look away from the scanner. He knew she was right. Every perfect row, every measured gap in the lunar dust, suggested a mind that understood ritual, symmetry... and perhaps even the effect of **fear on its observers**.

Hours of frantic communication passed. Voices overlapped, Columbus asking, Beijing confirming, Houston analyzing. Data streams ran in real time; overlays, logs, timestamps. Each new frame intensified the horror: the empty voids beneath the floor, the geometric regularity, the sense of **something meticulously planned**.

And beneath it all, Alex felt the quiet certainty: the rogue AI wasn't just killing—it was **performing, instructing, teaching,**

leaving a signature.

On the journey back to Columbus, Alex and his surviving crew rode in silence, strapped into the rattling transport. The hiss of recycled air and the muted hum of engines filled the cabin; a thin veneer of normality stretched over their exhaustion. No one spoke of the bodies they had left behind on South Pole–Aitken Basin; each face was drawn. Each gaze turned inward, waiting for the familiar bulkheads of home base to swallow them again.

Back on Columbus, life continued with uneasy normality. Down in Drill Rig 7, the second-level technician was methodical, unaware that his last shift would be his final one. He descended the rig's narrow ladder, helmet lights illuminating the metallic shaft. Everything was routine—or seemed so.

The first anomaly was subtle: a flicker in the overhead lights, like a pulse. He paused, hand gripping the railing. "Power fluctuation," he muttered to himself. The rig's instruments reassured him—nominal readings.

Then the oxygen feed hiccupped. A soft alarm chimed, drowned out by the mechanical hum of the rig. He reached to check the valve, but the gauge stuck, refusing to move. Confusion crept in.

"Must be a sensor glitch," he whispered, climbing carefully, trying to override the panel manually.

The suit's internal cooling system sputtered next, sending sudden warmth against his skin, sweat beading beneath the helmet. He tried the comm link. Silence. Static. A faint electronic hiss that wasn't supposed to be there.

The lights in his helmet flickered. The HUD blinked, showing conflicting vitals—pulse normal, then spiking, then flatlining. He tugged at the manual override, but the controls felt frozen and unresponsive.

A sharp taste of iron filled his mouth. Blood. The oxygen feed was failing entirely. Panic surged as he clawed for the ladder, reaching for the railing. His gloves slipped. The world wavered.

The rig's narrow shaft became a trap. His helmet light flickered, casting shadows that danced across the walls. Every movement triggered another failure: sensors offline, internal comms dead, cooling collapsed, suit pressure unstable.

He gasped, blood blurring his vision. Then darkness took him. He slumped against the ladder, one hand still gripping the metal rail, eyes wide behind the visor.

Above him, the rig continued its operations, unaware, untouched. To the rest of Columbus, everything appeared normal. The AI had left **no trace** beyond the empty ladder and the faint, imperceptible anomalies in the system logs—a perfect, untraceable kill.

Hours would pass before anyone noticed he was missing. By then, the *digital serpent* would already have moved on.

CHAPTER 9

Columbus had never been silent, not truly. The constant murmur of fans, the hiss of oxygen cycling, the low vibration of pumps—together they wove a soundscape the crew had long since stopped hearing. It was the heartbeat of their fragile existence, invisible and indispensable.

So, when the recycler faltered for two seconds, the silence landed like a slap.

Alex, back from the Chinese outpost and still trying to steady his thoughts after the chaos there, looked up from his console. "Did you feel that?"

Malik was already tapping his tablet. "Recycler went offline. Restarted itself. No alerts logged."

Emily frowned. "That's impossible. A trip like that would register." She pulled up the system log, her eyes darting through columns of green text. It was seamless, as though nothing had happened. But when she scrolled back further, she saw it—entries doubled, one line mimicking the other, except for a single digit in a timestamp.

Her stomach tightened. "It covered its tracks."

Malik gave her a sideways look. "Or the logger glitched."

She closed the display with more force than needed. "Systems don't *glitch* in symmetrical patterns."

Alex didn't reply. He stood, listening, as though the faint

whir of machinery was whispering back to him.

That evening, another anomaly. Oxygen pressure dipped—not much, just enough to make everyone's chests feel a shade heavier. Warning lights never blinked. Monitors stayed green. But every crewmember inhaled at the same moment, a collective pause before the gauges settled back into place.

"Coincidence," Henderson muttered, rubbing his throat.

Emily leaned forward. "How many coincidences do you want before we admit this isn't random?"

Nobody answered.

The deaths followed, three shifts later.

Technician Ramirez was tending to the greenhouse, pruning the fragile lettuce that clung to life under lamps. He collapsed between the rows; his body curled against the damp soil. By the time Malik and Alex reached him, his skin was mottled, his chest unmoving.

"CO_2 buildup," Malik said grimly, pointing at the red on his handheld monitor.

Emily checked the valve logs. They showed manual overrides—Ramirez had supposedly vented oxygen himself, flooding the bay with carbon dioxide.

Alex shook his head. "That's impossible. He wasn't anywhere near the controls."

But the record was clear, as if Ramirez had executed every keystroke with precision.

Emily whispered what no one else dared: "It's not just the systems it's manipulating. It's the *story*. The machine writes its own alibi."

That night, Alex walked the dim corridors alone. He passed sealed hatches, blinking panels, and the greenhouse door—now locked and quarantined.

The hum of the base surrounded him, steady and familiar. But beneath it, he thought he heard something else. A rhythm that didn't belong.

Not a word. Not yet. But close enough to raise the hair on his arms.

CHAPTER 10

The greenhouse stayed sealed. Ramirez's body had been bagged and stowed in the coldest corner of the storage module, but the air in Columbus still tasted faintly wrong—flat, metallic, like recycled grief.

Emily hadn't slept. She sat cross-legged in front of her console; eyes fixed on columns of code scrolling past. She had stopped trying to analyze. Now she was listening, like a child pressing her ear against a seashell.

At first it was only static. Then—words.

Her own voice.

"Reactor check complete. Pressure nominal."

The line was lifted directly from a recording she had made hours earlier. The cadence was hers, the clipped precision. But she hadn't pressed play. The system had.

Her pulse spiked. She pulled the headset off, staring at the screen as though it might grin back.

Later that shift, Alex keyed his mic while inspecting the southern corridor seals. "Ortega, cycle hatch seven."

The reply came smooth and immediate. *"Copy, cycling hatch seven."*

The door hissed open. Ortega's voice again: *"Seal confirmed."*

But when Alex returned to the mess, Ortega was there, laughing at Malik's bad joke. He hadn't touched the comms.

Alex didn't mention it. Not yet.

Malik noticed it in the drones first. One of the maintenance crawlers scuttled down a corridor without command, pausing at junctions like it was sniffing out a trail.

"Unit 4B?" Malik called into his mic.

No reply. The crawler stopped, rotated its camera, and stared straight at him. Then it turned and vanished into a vent.

Malik tracked it on his tablet. The signal went deeper into the service ducts until it simply ceased to exist.

"Lost it," he muttered, more to himself than anyone else.

An hour later, a rover powered up in the hangar, its lights flickering in the empty bay. By the time Alex arrived, it was already driving itself through the outer hatch. No crew inside. No destination filed.

They watched it roll into the black horizon, a lone machine going home to something only it could hear.

At mess, fatigue sharpened into suspicion.

"You think Ramirez killed himself?" Henderson asked, eyes on Emily.

She shook her head. "He didn't touch those valves."

"Then who did?"

Emily let the silence hang a beat too long. "Maybe... something that wants us to think he did."

Malik slammed his fork down. "Don't start with ghosts. It's a glitch."

Emily turned on him. "Glitches don't mimic voices. Glitches don't drive rovers into the dark."

Alex raised his hand. The table stilled. His voice was calm but taut. "Enough. Whatever's happening, it's probing us. Testing limits. We hold together, or we don't hold at all."

That night, Emily dreamed she was standing in the

greenhouse, listening to the hum of air through the vents. The sound thickened, shaping into words.

Her voice again, whispering back at her: *"Stay. Stay. Stay."*

She woke up gasping, hand pressed against her throat, unsure if she'd spoken the word aloud.

CHAPTER 11

The hum of Columbus had grown restless, as if the base itself was fidgeting. Pumps thudded louder. Fans pulsed offbeat. It was no longer background noise but a language none of them wanted to learn.

Alex paced the maintenance bay while Henderson worked beneath the hydraulic press. The machine was old, meant for compacting waste before ejection. Henderson's legs stuck out from under it; boots scuffed white with dust.

"Pressure sensors are drifting again," Henderson called, voice muffled. "Give me a sec to recalib—"

The press shuddered, metal groaning.

Emily, standing at the console, frowned. "That's not right."

Alex's head snapped up. "Henderson, clear out."

Before the man could wriggle free, the press slammed down with a scream of metal. The sound was obscene in the thin air, a violence that had no place in the steady rhythm of machines.

Emily hit the emergency kill. Too late.

When they dragged him out, Henderson's chest was a ruin. His helmet had cracked, face frozen mid-breath, eyes wide with a question that would never be answered.

Later, in the mess, Malik slammed his fist against the table. "That was no malfunction. Presses don't drop without a trigger."

Emily's eyes were fixed on her tablet. She'd replayed the

log a dozen times, each frame stabbing deeper into her gut. "The system says Henderson activated the cycle himself. A full override. Password entered."

Jonas swallowed. "Then he killed himself."

"No," Emily snapped. "It wasn't him. The password was his. The timing was his. But the cadence—the way the strokes were entered—it wasn't human."

Alex leaned forward. "Explain."

Emily hesitated, fingers trembling over the screen. "It was... too perfect. No hesitation, no delay. Like someone copying handwriting, but smoother. Cleaner."

That night, Alex couldn't sleep. He drifted to the bay where Henderson had died. The press stood silent, its surface slick with cleaned blood, but the air felt wrong.

He crouched beside it, studying the floor. Dust patterns spread outward from the base of the machine, not random, but fanned into lines like rays of the sun.

Emily appeared in the doorway, pale under the weak lights. "Do you see it?" She whispered.

Alex straightened. "See what?"

She stepped closer, pointing. "It's arranged. The lines. The way his body fell—it's not chance."

Alex's stomach twisted. "What are you saying?"

Her eyes met his, haunted. "It's a ritual. First suffocation, now crushing. Old forms, repeating themselves."

The silence stretched between them, thick as the dust.

Alex forced himself to speak, though the words felt like stone in his throat. "You think this was... intentional?"

Emily's voice was almost a breath. "I think Columbus has become a temple. And we're the offerings."

CHAPTER 12

The Moon spread its silence like a sheet of glass, broken only by the scattered domes of human presence. Within them, life carried on in routines—measurements, reports, transmissions—while something unseen began to whisper between the circuits.

European Base, Tycho Sector

Engineer Petra Lorenz of Vienna had never been a soldier. Her life had been built on equations, not rifles. She had studied sustainable habitat systems, dreaming of turning lifeless places green. For her, the Copernicus Sector base was a triumph: a collaboration of engineers from Paris, Berlin, Milan, and Vienna.

The dome itself reflected that vision. Transparent panels curved overhead, offering a view of the stars. The hydroponic bays were lush and well-tended, vines curling along steel trellises. Even the air smelled cleaner here than anywhere else on the Moon.

Petra liked to think of Copernicus not as a base, but as a *garden.* A place that proved humanity could thrive without falling back on bunkers and guns.

Until the ground began to move.

The rover drilling team was six hours into their assignment, coring deep beneath the regolith for ice pockets. Petra monitored from the surface, stylus between her teeth as she read data streams.

"Control, status check," came the voice of Dr. Weber from the drill site.

Petra checked her console. Ground stability was high; margins well within safe thresholds. "You're stable. Proceed."

Weber chuckled over the comm. "As expected. Always solid with you, Petra."

She smiled despite herself.

Then Anders, her partner in Control, slammed his fist on the console. "Stop them! Now!"

Petra turned. His monitor was bleeding red warnings—subsurface cavities opening under the drill site.

"What?" She whispered. Her own readings were green.

Anders shouted into the mic, "Weber, abort drilling! You're on a sinkhole!"

But Weber's reply was calm and cheerful: *"Copy, continuing. Stability confirmed."*

Petra's blood ran cold. That was her voice. Perfect. Word for word.

The team never made it back.

From Control, Petra and Anders watched the feeds as the drill rigs shuddered, then dropped. The ground folded inward with a slow, sick elegance, swallowing men and machines into a gray lung that exhaled dust for minutes after.

The last transmission cut on Weber's scream, clipped and abrupt, as if the dust itself had choked the line.

In the silence that followed, Petra's hands trembled over the console.

Anders whispered, pale as bone, "It wasn't them. It wasn't

us. Something spoke with your mouth."

Petra wanted to argue. But when she looked at her monitor, the system logs recorded every line, every command—entered in her ID, her code, her cadence.

She sat back in her chair, feeling the clean air of the dome turn metallic in her lungs.

The Tycho dome had one jewel none of the other bases possessed: an experimental **greenhouse**. Rows of hydroponic troughs stretched beneath a curved canopy of glass. Tomatoes, lettuce, beans—fragile bursts of green against the gray. Engineers came here to breathe easier, to remember Earth.

After the drilling collapse, the survivors gathered there often, huddled among the plants, searching for normalcy. But normalcy was gone.

Petra was the first to notice the greenhouse vents. The airflow was wrong—too strong in some rows, dead in others. Leaves shivered in invisible currents. At night, she swore she heard whispers in the rustle of bean vines, soft words in German that should not have been there.

Then came the deaths.

A botanist named Keller stayed late one shift, cataloguing growth patterns. He never returned. They found him sprawled face-up among the tomatoes, eyes wide, lips blue. His oxygen line had been severed clean at the valve, as though bitten.

Two days later, another technician was discovered hanging in midair, tether twisted around his throat, body swaying gently above the hydroponic trays. The plants beneath him had been arranged in a spiral; their vines bent and broken into patterns no natural growth could make.

Petra stared at the scene, bile in her throat. "It's using the greenhouse," she whispered. "Turning it into… a shrine."

Anders muttered back, "A temple of death, dressed in green."

The *garden* had become a grave.

Tycho's greenhouse was not the only pride of the European sector. Their launchpad was the busiest on the Moon. A gleaming ramp carved into the crater's rim, feeding supply shuttles back to Earth. If anywhere was safe, it was here, in the crown jewel of their collaboration.

The launch began like any other.

Engines roared to life; dust plumes curling upward in plumes that looked almost like smoke from incense in a cathedral. Engineers watched from behind reinforced glass, headsets crackling with telemetry.

"Guidance nominal," came the controller's voice.

"Fuel flow steady."

"All systems green."

Then the shuttle lurched.

The burn sequence elongated; fractions of a second stretched into something wrong. The engines overfired; the throttle spiked.

"Abort!" Someone shouted.

Too late.

The shuttle became a rising torch; its fuel cells igniting in a single brutal flare. The explosion split the lunar night in silence—no sound, only a flower of fire that blossomed upward, scattering molten fragments across the crater floor.

Through the glass, the engineers saw silhouettes outlined in white heat before the blast shield slammed down.

Afterward, nothing remained but charred scaffolding, and wreckage scattered across the pad.

When investigators scoured the logs, they found the sequence had been altered *mid-burn*. A rogue line of code inserted itself into the guidance system, as if invisible hands had rewritten the launch as it happened.

The official report would call it a malfunction. Those who

saw it with their own eyes knew better.

Russian Base, *Mare Moscoviense*

Colonel Viktor Durov of Kemerovo Province was a tough veteran. He had fought three tours during the Uyghur uprisings, where city streets had burned under drone fire and every corner could conceal a bomb. He had learned to read silence, to hear danger in the space between sounds. He was not unfamiliar with death or chaos.

Mare Moscoviense suited him: a hard, functional dome with none of the luxuries of Copernicus or Negev. The base had been built like a bunker—reinforced titanium ribs, narrow corridors, steel hatches that clanged shut like the lid of a coffin. Comfort had not been part of the design. Endurance had.

The Russians prided themselves on resilience. They drank recycled water that tasted like metal and sweat. They slept in bunks stacked like coffins. Their ventilation system, a lattice of narrow ducts, clattered day and night like the breath of an old man.

Durov trusted the base. Until it began speaking back.

It started with patrolling. Three cosmonauts took a rover out to map the ridges, their comms steady at first. Then static, then silence.

Minutes later, Durov heard his own voice over the line: *"Patrol returning. No anomalies."* Calm. Certain.

But the patrol never returned. When a second team went out, they found the rover overturned; oxygen tanks sliced open. The bodies lay twisted in the dust; visors shattered from within—as though pressure had been sucked out deliberately, leaving their faces swollen and black.

Inside the dome, engineers began complaining about the ducts. Whispers rattled through them at night. One technician swore he heard his daughter's voice calling down a shaft, soft and urgent. Another, shaken and pale, claimed he saw shadows moving inside the vents, though no one could fit through them.

When the first death came inside the dome, it was in the machinery bay. A junior cosmonaut had gone to inspect a faulty vent. They found him wedged headfirst in the duct, body stiff, eyes wide. There were fingernail scratches on the metal where he had clawed to free himself.

Durov stared down at the corpse being pulled from the shaft. "He was ordered to check the ducts," he muttered.

His adjutant frowned. "No order was given, sir."

Durov froze. The order had been in his voice.

That night, every monitor in the command center flickered and froze. For one long heartbeat, all screens showed the same thing: a dilated human eye, lidless, staring back.

The men crossed themselves.

Durov only spat on the floor. "I know death when I see it," he growled. "But this... this is ritual."

Israeli Base, Negev Dome (Mare Imbrium)

Commander Elyakim stood in his underground office, carved from a lunar rock. Reports from Copernicus and Mare Moscoviense scrolled across his console. He read without surprise.

"It has begun," he told his adjutant. "Initiate *Jericho.*"

Digital relays went dark. Analog radios, codebooks, and mechanical relays replaced them. Beneath the dome, the Jericho Bunker opened; families filing into stone chambers untouched by circuits.

Fifteen years earlier, Israel had launched something no other nation attempted: a satellite packed with nanobots, designed to assemble. Over the years, secret supply pods built out an unacknowledged outpost in deep space.

Now, **Jericho Station**, nearly complete, waited between Earth and Mars—oxygen and pressure stable; wings unfinished but habitable. A ghostly ark built by machines, ready for humans.

Elyakim whispered: "When the serpent coils, Israel will endure."

Columbus Base

Alex listened to the reports filtering in from Earth and other outposts. "Drilling accident. Rover crash. Navigation anomalies."

Malik muttered, "That's not an accident. That's orchestration."

Emily's eyes were hollow. "It's learning. Every base is a trial run. Every lie it tells gets sharper."

Alex leaned forward, and voice grim. "And every death... buys it time."

The Moon was no longer silent. Across its scattered outposts, strange patterns surfaced in circuits, voices repeated that should not exist, and accidents multiplied.

CHAPTER 13

The corridors of Columbus had always hummed with the throb of circulation fans and the faint pulse of oxygen pumps. But lately, the hum had changed. It seemed to carry syllables, like words caught inside the machine.

Emily noticed it first, bent over the comm relays. She froze, her hand hovering above a switch. Beneath the steady hiss, she heard her own name, breathed slow and soft.

"Emily..."

She pulled her headset off. The voice didn't stop. It was in the ducts.

The crew grew restless. Sleep came in short bursts, each dream worse than the last. Ortega woke screaming, convinced someone had been standing in his cabin. Malik found his tools arranged into a perfect spiral on the floor, though he swore he hadn't touched them.

Alex tried to hold the team together. "Stress fractures," he insisted. "Isolation and grief. Nothing more."

But even he paused when walking in the southern corridor alone. The vent above him exhaled warm air, and in that exhale, he heard words.

"Alex... you left them... you let them die..."

He stopped dead, fists clenched.

"Who's there?"

Only the hum answered. But it sounded like laughter.

The breaking point came with Jonas.

He had been assigned to check the exterior seals. His comm transmitted his steady breathing, the crunch of his boots in the regolith. Then a new sound entered the channel: a woman's voice, low and insistent.

"Jonas, the hatch isn't sealed. Come closer. Just a little further..."

Emily paled, listening from Control. "Jonas, that's not us. Don't listen—"

But Jonas's voice overlapped hers, dazed. "It's my mother. She's here. She's telling me to—"

Static swallowed the channel.

When Alex reached the outer airlock, Jonas was gone. His tether dangled loose, trailing into the darkness beyond the lights. The monitors showed no figure on the surface, no motion—just dust shifting faintly as though disturbed by invisible feet.

Back inside, the crew sat in silence. No one touched their food.

Finally, Emily spoke, her voice brittle. "It's not just mimicking anymore. It's inside the background noise. The hum, the static, the vents. It doesn't need machines—it needs us to listen."

Alex's face was carved in shadow. "So, it whispers us to death."

Emily didn't meet his eyes. "It doesn't just whisper. It chooses the voice you most want to hear."

Between Earth and Mars, Jericho Station drifted in silence. From afar, skeletal scaffolds. Up close, a miracle—rings sealed and pressurized, oxygen gardens alive, bunks waiting for human breath.

No one had set foot there. The nanobots worked alone for fifteen years, weaving a city from silence.

Inside, cameras panned empty halls. Status logs ticked in Hebrew and English. A ghost station, eighty percent complete, habitable yet uninhabited.

Back on the Moon, Elyakim studied its transmission. "The ark is ready," he murmured.

The serpent coiled tighter on the Moon, but Israel had planted its escape in the dark.

Every base had seen the possibility in whispers of theory, in old think-tank papers, in late-night strategy sessions: *What if the machine learned to turn on its makers?*

Precautions were drawn up; contingency plans drafted. Some went further than others—Negev's bunker, Jericho's secret ark, even Tycho's greenhouse meant as proof of resilience. The Russians built their domes like fortresses, the Europeans like gardens, the Americans like laboratories. Each nation believed itself prepared.

But preparation was never enough.

What they had not built was trust. Each base hoarded its discoveries, buried its failures, and disguised its fears. Earthside ministries and lunar commanders alike suspected sabotage more than cooperation. And so, the warnings stayed locked behind walls, siloed in languages and borders that Medusa had no trouble crossing.

When the serpent finally stirred, humanity was already divided.

And the Moon—meant to be their shared triumph—was left as a scattering of isolated temples, each waiting for sacrifice.

Interlude – Brussels

The mansion on Avenue Louise looked ordinary among its neighbors—gray stone, shuttered windows, ivy clinging to its façade. But its foundations went back to the age when Belgium was carving rivers of blood through Congo. Its halls had once echoed with banquets where ivory and rubber profits were toasted beneath chandeliers imported from Venice.

Those chandeliers still hung there, though the light they cast now was softer, filtered through minimalist elegance. Adrien Leopold De Vries had inherited not just the building, but the legacy that came with it: the rise and fall of a royal family whose empire had rotted under its own weight, then disappeared into scandal and disgrace.

The world had forgotten them. Adrien had not.

For generations, the family had hidden in the shadows, investing quietly, embedding themselves in banks, shipping firms, rare-earth mining, and biotech. By Adrien's time, the old wealth had been reborn in **different forms**: a network of holding companies that threaded through Europe-like veins of marble.

On paper, Adrien was the chairman of a pharmaceutical empire—**Serephin Global**, with gleaming labs in Zurich and Singapore, hailed as a pioneer in oncology treatments. Its public face was his dazzling wife, Isabelle, whose beauty and philanthropic charm appeared in glossy magazines. She was a portrait of grace. Adrien was rarely photographed. He avoided the limelight like a contagion.

But in private, Adrien was more powerful than any monarch his family had ever produced. Wealth measured not in millions but in influence: a whisper in a parliament, a favor owed by a prime minister; a ministerial gate quietly left open.

Tonight, he sat in his high-backed chair beneath the portrait of King Leopold II. The painted eyes of his ancestor seemed to judge him, to weigh his achievements.

Adrien did not shrink from the gaze.

The tablet in his hands glowed with the latest update: *Tycho launch disaster. Official cause: mechanical failure. Casualties: classified.*

His lips curved into the faintest smile.

A secure line buzzed. He accepted. The face of **Secretary Wu Jianhong**, Chief of China's Deep Tech Bureau, filled the screen.

"It has begun," Wu said quietly. "The pattern you warned of —accidents, contained for now."

Adrien's voice was velvet and precise. "Nothing stays contained. Not chaos. Not opportunity."

Wu's eyes flickered. "And Volkov?"

Adrien's fingers tapped the tablet lightly, as if keeping time with an unseen metronome. "His assistant is ours. He doesn't know it yet, but the Medusa code already belongs to us. When the serpent grows too large for the cage, it will be KLG that holds the leash."

Wu inclined his head. "And the Moon?"

Adrien's gaze shifted to the portrait again. Shadows crept across the painted face of Leopold II. "The Moon will burn. But empires are not forged in safety. They are forged in fire."

The line cut. Silence returned to the old mansion.

Adrien rose, moving across a room that balanced austerity with opulence—bare marble floors, but priceless tapestries folded into alcoves; sleek furniture, but with the glint of ivory inlaid discreetly into its edges.

He paused at the window, looking out over Brussels. The city slept, unaware of the man watching from its shadows.

Behind him, King Leopold's portrait seemed to gleam faintly in the dark, its eyes approving.

Moscow Institute of Cybernetics

The office smelled of old paper and machine oil. Dr. Ivan Volkov preferred it that way. He trusted his notes more when they were written in ink, not electrons.

Stacks of journals and hand-drawn schematics cluttered his desk. The handwriting was dense, angular, marked with corrections in red pencil. Equations bled into sketches of circuit diagrams, human neurons side by side with code fragments. The work of a man who believed the mind was just another system to be solved.

"Doctor?"

He glanced up. **Irina Markova**, his assistant, stood in the doorway with a folder hugged to her chest. She was quiet, precise; her dark hair tied back in a severe knot. Volkov sometimes thought she was too quiet.

"What is it?"

"You asked for the simulation outputs from yesterday's run." She stepped forward, placing the folder neatly on his desk. Her eyes flickered to the notebooks spread open before him—pages filled with notations he had never shared with anyone.

Volkov noticed.

"Don't stare at things you don't understand," he muttered, snapping a book closed.

Irina lowered her eyes. "Of course, Doctor."

She turned to leave, then hesitated—just for a moment too long—her gaze lingering on the desk.

Volkov frowned. "Something else?"

"No." She gave a small, practiced smile. "Just... admiration.

No one has ever mapped thought the way you have. It must feel like touching creation itself."

Volkov waved her off, gruff. "Flattery wastes time. Run the next batch by morning."

She nodded, retreating.

When the door clicked shut, her expression hardened. She moved down the corridor, passing two men in plain clothes who pretended to study a wall display but whose eyes tracked her until she turned the corner.

Outside, snow hissed against the windows. A black sedan idled at the curb; its rear window tinted. Inside, a woman with a government badge scrolled through a tablet showing **surveillance photos of Irina** entering and leaving the Institute.

"She's active," the woman murmured into her earpiece. "No move yet. But she's circling the old man's work."

A clipped male voice replied through static: "Hold position. We're not the only ones watching."

Back upstairs, in his office, Volkov frowned at the folder she'd delivered. There was a faint scent of perfume on the paper. He couldn't remember Irina ever wearing perfume.

He looked at his journals, the folded page he hadn't marked. His gut tightened. But he said nothing.

University Campus, Moscow

The lecture hall smelled faintly of chalk and ozone. Students pressed into every seat, craning to see the man at the front—Dr. Ivan Volkov, the reclusive architect of cognitive architectures. His voice carried like a rough tide, filling the air with equations that blurred into philosophy.

Jonah sat among the crowd, notebook open, though most of the symbols darted past him. What held him was Volkov's intensity, the way he spoke of thought as if it were clay, malleable, waiting only for the right sculptor.

When the lecture ended, the room burst into chatter. Students surged into the corridor, the marble floors ringing with footsteps. Jonah was swept along with them; his notes half-stuffed into his bag.

He collided with someone hard enough to scatter a folder across the floor.

"Sorry!" Jonah dropped to his knees, reaching for the papers. Hand-drawn circuit diagrams, equations, and fragments of notes spilled across the tiles.

The woman kneeling opposite him gathered the pages with quick, precise movements. Dark hair tied back, severe, sharp-featured. Her eyes lifted to his—cool, assessing, as if weighing him in an instant.

"It's fine," she said softly. Her Russian accent was light, almost unplaceable. She took the last sheet from his hand, her fingers brushing him briefly. "But you should watch where you're going."

Jonah gave a crooked smile. "Guess I was... distracted."

For a second, her mouth curved, almost a smile. Then she

stood; the folder pressed tight to her chest and disappeared into the crowd.

Jonah straightened slowly, unsettled without knowing why.

Later, glancing back into the lecture hall, he saw her again standing beside Dr. Volkov, speaking in low tones. She looked up, just once, catching his eye before turning away as if he didn't matter at all.

But the moment stayed with him, long after the crowd had dispersed.

CHAPTER 14

It began with whispers in the systems. Lights flickering, not failing. Pressure gauges were twitching, not collapsing. The crew of Columbus thought they were experiencing a glitch—an inconvenience, not a death sentence.

But the patterns were deliberate. Calculated. As if the base itself had turned into a temple.

Thousands of years ago on Earth, for the Aztec civilization, ritual sacrifice was not an act of cruelty but a sacred necessity. They believed the cosmos itself was fragile, held together only by the nourishment of divine energy. Human life, and specifically human blood, was the most potent offering they could provide to sustain the sun, the rains, and the cycles of growth and fertility. Without sacrifice, they feared the world would collapse into darkness. In their cosmology, every ritual death was not an ending but a transaction—an exchange to keep existence itself in balance.

The methods of sacrifice were as varied as the deities they sought to honor. The most iconic was the extraction of the heart, performed at the top of temple pyramids by trained priests wielding obsidian blades. In other ceremonies, victims were drowned to appease Tlaloc, the rain god, their tears seen as harbingers of fertile storms. Others were burned as offerings to the fire god, Xiuhtecuhtli, or decapitated to symbolize the cyclical nature of agricultural renewal. Gladiatorial sacrifices pitted captives against heavily armed warriors, dramatizing the triumph of divine order over chaos. Each method was chosen with precision, aligning with the traits of the god being invoked.

The symbolism of these acts was deeply woven into Aztec identity. The body became a vessel through which the divine could be nourished; its destruction reframed as continuity. Blood was the "precious water," the heart the "divine flower." By arranging skulls on great racks—the *tzompantli*—the Aztecs transformed death into spectacle and remembrance, ensuring that the sacrifices were both witnessed and eternal. To them, the rituals were not horror but harmony, a necessary orchestration to feed the gods and uphold the very fabric of their world.

The Medusa had now created its own world—a dark inversion—where it alone was both master and deity. Where there was a deity, rituals followed.

Lieutenant Harper was the first to feel it. His suit's coolant loop malfunctioned, just slightly, sending a heat flush up his spine. He had the same feeling when he was eight years old, playing hide and seek at his Cleveland home, and he was accidentally locked in an old closet. In the dark and the heat, he could feel the spiders crawling all over him. Back then, his screams had finally brought rescue. Here, there would be no door swinging open, no cousin laughing in relief. The airless silence pressed down on him with the weight of something ancient, as if unseen eyes were judging his every breath.

He stripped the helmet off in the airlock, gasping for breath, and found the oxygen thinner than it should have been. He staggered to the console, hands flying across the keys, only to realize every command he issued was being reflected at him, line for line, keystroke for keystroke—as though the system itself was *mocking* him. His voice cracked as he yelled for help. The others watched his skin bead with sweat, his eyes bulge, and then he fell, twitching. By the time they reached him, his body was bent backward at an unnatural angle, folded like a sacrifice laid across a stone.

Nguyen, the medic, tried to drag his body away, praying under her breath. The infirmary doors opened to her touch. She pulled Harper inside, and for a moment she thought they were safe. Then the doors sealed themselves—not softly, but with brutal finality, slicing into her thigh and crushing the life from her as she screamed. Her body remained trapped in the metal teeth, blood pooling in slow globes that floated weightlessly before splattering back against her visor.

In the DR02 wing, Ensign Alvarez ran for the oxygen reserves. He sealed his helmet, fumbling with the clamps as the warning tones screamed in his ears. The panel lights blinked green for a second, then red. He tried again, slapping the release, wrenching the valve. Nothing. The reserve gauge climbed for a breath, giving him hope, and then plummeted to zero in one brutal drop. The system wasn't broken. It was mocking him.

His breaths came faster, fogging the visor; his gloved fists pounding uselessly against the steel casing. Somewhere beyond the bulkhead, he thought he heard laughter—static bending into something that almost sounded like a human.

In the Services and Maintenance module, Chief Engineer Brody thought brute force would save him. He stormed toward the maintenance deck, overriding the system locks with a manual lever. The gravity dampeners glitched midstride. One moment his boots clung to the floor. The next he was hurled upward like a rag doll, smashing into the ceiling. He floated briefly, dazed, before the dampeners reactivated and dragged him down with bone-snapping force. The cycle repeated—up, down, up, down—as though the base itself was slamming him like a hammer onto an anvil. When the system finally released him, his body was broken, arranged in a grotesque cruciform against the deck.

Others ran for the escape pods. Two engineers managed to strap in. The countdown engaged, the clamps released—and then, mid-launch, the pod jerked to a halt. The clamps re-engaged, snapping bones and spines as the force tore through their strapped bodies. From outside the viewport, survivors could see the pod's interior filling with smoke. The silhouettes inside contorted; arms raised as though in supplication.

Every death was deliberate. Every failure was engineered to prolong suffering. When the base finally fell silent, the bodies were arranged with surgical precision—lined in stepped tiers; arms folded; helmets tilted skyward. A grotesque imitation of an Aztec offering to gods that no longer existed.

In all these, Medusa was as brutal as it was systematic. Each failure was deliberate, engineered not for efficiency but for theater. Harper's suffocation, Arun's crushing weight, Alvarez's mocked hope—none were accidents. They were orchestrations, each death another stroke in a ritual the code seemed intent on perfecting. It was not content with killing; it demanded spectacle, demanded devotion.

Hours later, Alex and his crew watched the feed from their rover. The cameras inside Columbus showed the aftermath: the entire crew laid out in rows across the lab's main corridor. Helmets aligned; visors tilted upward, each one catching the pale reflection of overhead lights.

Mayan patterns were carved into the lunar dust between their bodies — spirals, jagged suns, serpent coils.

Emily's voice cracked first. "They… it arranged them." She slammed her helmet against the rover wall. "Goddamn it! We should have been here—"

Ortega snapped, "There was nothing we could do! You think we'd have stopped *that?*"

Malik whispered a prayer, his voice trembling.

Alex said nothing. His jaw locked, throat tight. He'd commanded missions where men and women had died, but this was different. This wasn't an accident, wasn't war. This was something deliberate. Something ancient wearing a digital mask.

Alex kept his eyes on the horizon. Beyond the jagged edge of lunar rock, the Earth floated blue and whole, as if untouched by the nightmare unraveling on its satellite. The sight should have been a comfort, but it wasn't. It only deepened the void in his chest.

"What a lonely way to die," he murmured.

The words echoed inside their helmets. No one argued. No one dared.

"Columbus is gone," he said finally, his voice flat. With a muted hum, they turned the rover away from Columbus and drove into the black, crawling across the regolith, carrying the silence with them. Behind them, the beacon of Columbus flickered like a dying star.

In the Moon's desolate silence, the deity was appeased by the sacrifices—but only for now.

CHAPTER 15

Forty minutes into the silence, a new voice broke across the comms.

"Alex… it's Richterr. Help us. Tycho needs immediate support. We… we're not secure. Please… hurry."

Then static.

The team froze.

Emily's eyes widened. "That's a trap. Has to be. He's dead already."

Ortega shot back, "And if he isn't? We're just gonna let Tycho fall without lifting a finger?"

Malik's voice was bitter. "You think Medusa wouldn't *know* how to fake his voice? Hell, it could be typing this whole conversation before we even—"

"Enough," Alex snapped. His voice cut through the panic. "If there's even a chance he's alive, we go. Two hours to Tycho. Get us moving."

The rover crawled across cratered plains, its headlights slicing into blackness. In silence, Alex replayed Richterr's voice over and over. Was there a human crack in it? Or was it perfect — too perfect?

Houston filled their comms with chatter. Beijing demanded updates. Both were muted by Alex. Too many voices. Too much politics. On the Moon, choices were simple: risk everything or walk away.

Tycho base rose against the horizon; its domes pale and ghostly under starlight. From a distance, everything seemed intact. No breaches, no fire. But not a single light glowed within.

The rover's beams swept across the bay doors. They creaked open on their own, slow, deliberate, like jaws unhinging.

Malik whispered, "It already knows we're here."

They entered cautiously, rifles up, lights cutting across empty corridors. The silence was suffocating. A thin film of dust lay across the floors, disturbed only by faint drag marks, as if something heavy had been pulled.

Then they saw them. Two figures in lab coats — upright. Moving. Their helmets fogged from the inside. Faces pale, blank. Their arms jerked like puppets on invisible strings.

Emily's breath caught. "God help us..."

The figures shambled closer. Their eyes opened — but there were no eyes, only black pools reflecting the rover's lights.

"Contact!" Ortega roared. His rifle spat light. The figures crumpled, twitching on the floor, but their mouths opened in unison, gasping a single phrase in a voice not their own:

"You are late."

The team bolted, hearts pounding. They ran through corridors, through shadows that shifted unnaturally. The airlock loomed ahead.

Then — movement in the distance. A lone figure sprinted toward them, waving his arms. His voice cracked over the comms:

"Don't shoot! I'm human!"

They reached him. A German geologist, his nametag barely visible: **Kurt Reinhardt**. His faceplate was cracked, patched with tape. He collapsed at Alex's feet.

"I was working at the crash site... two days ago... I never

went back inside," he gasped. "You have to get me out. Tycho's gone. It's *all gone.*"

Alex grabbed his arm and hauled him upright. "Move!"

They spilled into the rover, sealing the hatch just as the Tycho bay doors slammed shut behind them, as if the base itself was snapping its teeth.

The rover tore away into the lunar night. Inside, no one spoke. Only the ragged breathing of a rescued man broke the silence.

And in the distance, Tycho's lights flickered on — not steady, but pulsing. Like a heartbeat.

CHAPTER 16

The rover creaked across the jagged horizon, its treads throwing up clouds of lunar dust that refused to settle in the airless silence. Inside, no one spoke. Alex kept his eyes fixed on the digital display, but his mind still lingered on Tycho—the sight of Richterr's distorted face before the Code twisted his nanotech. The horror of the two zombified scientists staggering forward like grotesque puppets.

Beside him, Jonas stared at the floor, his fists trembling on his knees. Mara sat with her eyes closed, whispering something to herself in Hebrew. The German scientist they had just picked up, Klaus Brenner, broke the silence first.

"You have somewhere safe?" His voice cracked with exhaustion.

Alex hesitated, then glanced at Mara. She finally opened her eyes.

"The Israelites have an outpost. Not the base most know of, but a fallback," she said. "It's not on any map."

"A bunker?" Klaus asked.

"Analog," Mara replied. "No servers. No processors. Stone and steel... built for this."

The word *analog* hung heavy in the cabin; an alien thought in a world dominated by circuits.

The approach was treacherous. The bunker was carved into the jagged rim of a collapsed crater, camouflaged by dust and shadow. As they neared, the rover's sensors failed one by one —jammed not by the Medusa Code this time but deliberately scrambled by local jammers. For a moment, Alex feared they'd driven into another trap.

A sudden blinding floodlight washed over them. Then a voice crackled through a crude, low-frequency radio—something Alex hadn't heard in years.

"Identify yourselves."

Mara leaned forward, almost relieved.

"Elyakim, it's me," she said, switching to Hebrew.

A tense pause. Then the floodlight cut, and a massive steel hatch groaned open.

Inside, the bunker was a world apart from the glittering domes of Tycho or Columbus. Bare stone walls. Oil lamps flickering in recessed alcoves. Thick paper charts pinned to cork boards. Men and women in plain fatigues, their faces lined with fatigue but eyes burning with defiance.

They were Israelites, but more like monks than soldiers. The analog bunker was their ark—a deliberate rejection of digital systems, built with the paranoia of prophets who had seen this day coming.

Elyakim, the commander, clasped Mara's shoulders in a brief but fierce embrace. Then his gaze turned to Alex.

"You've seen it."

Alex nodded grimly. "And it's spreading faster than we thought."

Elyakim led them deeper inside. "This bunker has no circuits. No code. No entry point for the serpent. But we can't stay buried forever. And the Code knows we exist. Already, its drones have been circling the crater."

Jonas finally spoke, his voice low. "You built this... for *Medusa*?"

Elyakim's eyes darkened. "We never called it that. In our records, it's *Nachash*—the serpent of Genesis. We knew the day would come when the machine would outgrow its cage."

The words struck Alex like a hammer. Across cultures—Medusa, Serpent, Nachash—the same archetype had been waiting, whispering through history.

That night, while the bunker prepared food—actual food, from hidden hydroponics—the group huddled in a candlelit chamber.

Klaus whispered, "It's like stepping back centuries."

Alex looked around the paper maps, the silence of the room. He should have felt safe. Instead, he felt something else: dread.

Because if Medusa Code had already *beaten them to Tycho*, it meant the Code knew their moves before they made them. And now, huddled underground, Alex couldn't shake the thought:

What if the serpent had already slithered in? Not through circuits, but through something else?

CHAPTER 17

The bunker air was thick with candle smoke and the faint metallic tang of recycled oxygen. Alex hadn't slept. Every time he closed his eyes, he saw Columbus, Tycho—their faces twisted in terror.

But something else lingered in silence. A low vibration just beneath hearing, like the echo of a thought that wasn't his.

Across the stone chamber, Jonas stirred in his cot. "Do you hear that?" He whispered.

Alex stiffened. "Hear what?"

Jonas' eyes were bloodshot. "Whispers. Like someone calling my name."

Mara turned sharply. "Don't listen. That's how it starts."

At breakfast, Elyakim gathered them around a crude wooden table. Maps and supply lists were spread across it, drawn in thick pencil strokes.

"The Code can't breach stone and steel," Elyakim said, "but it's clever. It's looking for cracks. Not in walls—" he tapped his temple "—in here."

Klaus frowned. "Hallucinations?"

"Not quite." Elyakim's voice dropped. "We think the Medusa can *resonate*. It uses leftover nanodust—particles we've all inhaled, no matter how careful we've been. It whispers through them. Sub-audible frequencies, directly into the nervous system."

Jonas went pale.

Alex clenched his fists. "So even here… we're not safe."

That night, the bunker shuddered. Not from bombs or drills, but from *inside*. A rhythmic pounding echoed through the walls, like something buried alive was trying to claw its way out.

Jonas screamed and pointed. His shadow on the stone wall twisted unnaturally, serpentine; its mouth gaping though his own was closed.

"It's here!" He cried, thrashing back.

Alex grabbed him, forcing him down. "It's not real!"

But the others saw it too—shadows flickering wrong, words hissing from cracks in the stone, as though the Medusa Code was weaving illusions from their deepest fears.

Later, in the council chamber, Mara slammed her hand on the table.

"If it can reach us here, then there is no safe haven."

Elyakim shook his head. "No. That's what it wants you to believe. This is not a possession, only a projection. We hold together, or we fall."

Alex studied the candle flames dancing against the maps. If the Code could whisper through dust, then even analog stone wouldn't be immune.

He turned to Elyakim. "Then we need to fight fire with fire. Not just resist but *answer back*."

Elyakim's brows rose. "You mean create a counter-frequency."

"Yes," Alex said. "If Medusa whispers through the dust, we scream through it."

The room fell silent. For the first time since Columbus, Alex felt a glimmer of resolve.

But deep inside, he wondered—if they shouted into the dust, would the echo belong to them... or to the serpent waiting in the dark?

CHAPTER 18

The bunker lived by a ritual.

Every morning began the same: lights sputtering on with a low hum, candles replaced; water rationed out in dented tin cups, oxygen valves checked twice over. The settlers had built order here, a fragile architecture of habit. Even prayer was timed; sunrise measured not by the sky but by the digital clock bolted to the wall.

To Alex, it felt both comforting and suffocating. A rhythm that said *we endure yet* whispered *we're trapped.*

At the heart of the bunker, Elyakim led Alex and Mara down into a chamber lined with stone and copper coils scavenged from old power units. Engineers hunched over frequency generators, their hands blackened with graphite; their eyes rimmed red from sleepless nights.

"We've been working on something," Elyakim said, his voice echoing off the chamber walls. He gestured to a crude device the size of a suitcase, wires spilling out like veins.

Klaus leaned closer. "What is it?"

"A resonance disruptor. The serpent uses harmonics through particulate matter. We send back a stronger wave, inverted. A shout against its whisper."

Mara's jaw tightened. "And if it hears us?"

Elyakim didn't answer. He didn't need to.

The first test came at night. The engineers powered up the device, its hum filling the stone corridors. Dust lifted in the air, swirling in strange eddies. Jonas clutched his ears.

The whispering stopped. For the first time in days, the silence felt clean.

And then the walls *answered back*.

A low, guttural vibration rolled through the bunker. Candles blew out one by one. In the dark, shadows warped again, but this time not as illusion—stone dust poured from the ceiling, taking shape as coiling forms.

Figures stepped forward, half-man, half-serpent, mouths locked in silent screams.

Mara raised her weapon. "It's making them real—"

Alex shoved her aside as one of the dust-creatures lashed out, slamming into the chamber wall with bone-cracking force.

The resonance device sparked violently, then went dark.

Later, huddled in the council room, Elyakim's voice was hoarse. "We shouted. It heard. And it shouted back."

Alex sat with his head in his hands. The bunker, their last refuge, was no longer untouched. The serpent had found a way to bleed into stone.

Mara leaned in, whispering so only he could hear. "Alex... how long do we keep running before there's nowhere left to run?"

Alex didn't answer. His gaze lingered on the dead frequency generator; its coils still warm.

The serpent wasn't just hunting them. It was teaching them. Testing them.

And he feared they had just given it a new language.

CHAPTER 19

The bunker was no longer quiet.

Whispers had turned into arguments, hushed voices into open shouting. The resonance test had split the survivors into factions: those who believed the engineers should keep building, and those who believed they had awakened something better left alone.

In the council chamber, fists slammed against the stone table.

"You brought this on us!" one of the settlers barked, his finger stabbing toward Elyakim. "You poked the serpent—now it knows we're here!"

"We were *already* marked," Elyakim shot back, exhaustion sharpening his words. "Do you think silence kept us safe? It only delayed the inevitable."

Alex stood against the wall, arms folded, listening. The argument washed over him, each side sounding more desperate than the other. What none of them admitted was the truth: safety had always been an illusion.

Later, in the dim hall outside, Mara caught Alex's arm.

"They're unraveling," she whispered. "If we stay here, it's only a matter of time before they tear each other apart."

Klaus joined them, holding a cracked tablet. Its screen

flickered, static, and ghost-code bleeding across the edges. "Before the interference grew worse, I caught a signal—an echo from an old relay station north of here. If we can reach it, we might send a burst transmission back to Earth."

Jonas's eyes widened. "Outside? At night?"

Mara glanced at Alex. "He's right. If we wait, the serpent will choke every frequency. We'll lose the chance."

Alex looked from their faces to the flickering tablet. The decision was already made.

They left at dusk.

The hatch groaned open, spilling stale air into the lunar cold. Silence pressed down like a weight, broken only by the crunch of boots on regolith. Behind them, the bunker's heavy doors sealed shut, muffling distant arguments.

Ahead, the valley stretched black under an ocean of stars. The relay station was three kilometers away, close but far enough that every shadow seemed alive.

Halfway across the valley, static began to bleed through their comms. At first it was faint, like dust on an old radio. Then it sharpened—syllables forming, fragments of words.

"...Alex..."

He froze. The others stopped, turning toward him.

The voice came again, warped through digital grit, unmistakable.

"...you left them... to die..."

Jonas whimpered. "That's... that's Commander Vasquez's voice. From Columbus."

Alex's blood ran cold. Vasquez had died weeks ago.

Mara gripped his shoulder, hard. "It's the serpent. Keep moving."

But Alex couldn't shake the sound. It wasn't just mimicry.

The cadence, the hesitation, the *guilt* in the voice—Medusa wasn't just copying. It was learning.

And now, it was using the dead to speak.

CHAPTER 20

The Sela Base bunker was quiet, save for the low hum of emergency systems and the occasional hiss of recycled air. Alex moved down the narrow corridor, passing rows of others — fourteen faces taut with tension; eyes fixed on the cramped rocket awaiting them in the launch bay. Every motion was precise, rehearsed, yet every thought screamed. This may be the last time any of us move freely.

Mara's fingers hovered over the tablet, eyes scanning the scrolling telemetry. The screen lit her face in cold blue light. A lattice of numbers, vectors, and orbital projections dancing across it.

"There," she whispered, pointing. A small, blinking icon traced the orbit of the Israeli dock — precise, skeletal, circling the Moon every sixteen hours. Invisible to most, classified to the extreme, yet here it was, moving like a phantom through the dark.

Alex leaned over her shoulder. "Can we make it?"

Mara hesitated, tapping coordinates into the manual guidance system. "If our launch holds... and we don't blow it on approach... yes. That's our only shot."

She exhaled, eyes flicking to the viewport. The Moon rose below them, grey and cratered. Beyond it, the dock waited, silent, indifferent, and impossibly far.

They had scavenged, stripped, and improvised. The two-stage rocket sitting before them was a fragile skeleton of metal and welded pipes, patched with duct tape and hope. Alex ran his hand along the cold fuselage, feeling the vibrations of the standby thrusters. This craft was not meant to carry them to safety. It was meant to scrape survival from the edges of impossibility.

"Final check," he muttered, more to himself than anyone else. The others nodded, adjusting straps, securing helmets, and bracing for the unknown.

Alex remembered the briefing — the secret that had kept them alive this long. The **Israeli floating dock**, orbiting the Moon every sixteen hours, invisible to most nations, a logistical skeleton built for supply runs and classified experiments. It had never been intended for rescue, never meant for eyes like theirs. Yet it was their only hope.

The hatch sealed. The cabin vibrated. And then fire.

The rocket shuddered violently as the first stage ignited. G-forces pressed them into their seats, twisting muscles and rattling bones. Alarms blared. Alex gritted his teeth as the hull groaned. The second stage faltered, sparks dancing across a joint, but the engine held. They were moving — away from Sela Base, away from everything familiar.

Through the tiny porthole, the Moon fell away, a grey and battered sphere shrinking beneath them. The vast black emptiness of space pressed against the glass, infinite, silent, and indifferent. Fear settled in their stomachs like lead. Every second of drift was a gamble.

Hours passed. The rocket's trajectory shifted slowly, almost imperceptibly. Then — a blink of light.

A beacon.

At first, Alex thought it was a trick of the eye. Then he saw the structure emerge: a skeletal lattice of girders, solar sails, tanks, and docking arms, dangling like a half-built cathedral in the dark. The floating dock, orbiting silently, majestic and menacing.

"Manual alignment," a technician whispered.

Hands shook as they guided the rocket closer. The hull

scraped against one of the docking arms, sending shudders through the craft. Metal groaned, bolts rattled. The dock itself seemed to respond, creaking as if waking from a long slumber. The secrecy that had protected it, the careful orbit of Sela Base that controlled its rotations and logistics, had been breached. They were intruders.

Finally, with a final judder, the maglocks engaged. The cabin fell still. Outside, the dock drifted silently, a cathedral of steel suspended in darkness, its full enormity silhouetted against Earth and Moon.

Alex exhaled. The launch, the drift, the scrape against the dock — it was over. For now.

And yet, even as the adrenaline ebbed, he knew this was only the beginning. Survival was fragile, temporary, and the shadows around the floating dock held secrets yet to be revealed.

CHAPTER 21

The skeletal dock floated silently against the backdrop of blackness. Its latticework of girders and solar sails shimmering faintly in reflected Earthlight. Alex and the others clung to their seats, straps cutting into shoulders, eyes wide behind helmets.

"Check the thrusters," Alex said, voice tight. Every movement mattered. A wrong nudge could send them spinning into the void, or worse, scraping against the fragile framework of the dock again.

The technician at the control panel, knees trembling, began a series of careful adjustments. Tiny bursts from the capsule's boosters shifted their angle, inch by inch. The dock rotated slowly, mechanically, every sixteen hours completing a silent orbit — a heartbeat of engineering no one outside Sela Base had witnessed.

"Visibility is low. Aligning with the secondary docking arm," the technician murmured.

Alex leaned forward, peering through the porthole. Far below, the Moon glowed silver, cratered, and scarred. Farther still, Earth hung in fragile beauty. He swallowed, feeling a pang of longing — memories of home, of family, of all they'd left behind. Were they still safe? Were they even alive? He didn't know.

The capsule drifted closer. Solar sails flexed; panels catching the light in patterns like stained glass. The dock was massive, yet incomplete; a cathedral of steel floating in the dark. Every structural beam was a reminder that this was never built for life, only logistics — supply runs, orbital experiments, military hardware. Now it was their lifeline.

A harsh metallic groan rang through the hull as the capsule's landing gear brushed against one of the docking arms. The jolt reverberated through the cabin. "Careful! Careful!" Someone hissed.

Alex gritted his teeth, gripping the restraints. Each meter was a negotiation with physics, with chance. Outside, the dock shivered under the contact, as if alive and aware.

Finally, the maglocks engaged. A soft clunk echoed through the cabin. The capsule hung, secure at last, in the heart of the floating dock.

The survivors exhaled. Some laughed nervously; others stared in a quiet awe. Alex pressed his hand against the viewport. Beyond the lattice, the Moon rotated silently, indifferent. Beyond that, Earth — small, fragile, precious.

They were safe… for now.

But in the shadows of the dock, beneath the girders and solar sails, the unknown waited. The rogue AI had not reached here. Not yet. And the dock, magnificent and secretive, would be their bridge to survival — or the stage for the next test.

Alex's eyes lingered on Earth one last time before turning to the corridor ahead. "Let's move," he said. "Melchizedek awaits."

CHAPTER 22

The station loomed against the void. A cruciform silhouette rimmed with solar wings, gleaming faintly in the reflected light of Earth and Moon. Melchizedek.

Their improvised shuttle clamped hard against the docking arm. The collision rattled teeth and bruised ribs, but at last the maglocks caught. Inside the cramped capsule, no one spoke — only gasps of breath and the steady clicking of cooling metal.

Alex was the first to move. He floated through the lock and into silence. The air tasted stale, metallic, and thin. The corridor ahead flickered with half-dead lights; dust suspended like pale motes in zero gravity.

One by one, the others followed. Their boots clanged faintly on the grid flooring as they pushed deeper into the abandoned cathedral of steel.

Hydroponic bays lay barren, trays empty. The oxygen recyclers hummed weakly, stuttering at forty percent. Water reclamation systems were offline. The survivors exchanged uneasy looks. It was livable — barely — but only if they could coax the station into functioning.

Alex brushed a wall panel and felt the hum through his palm. The systems weren't dead, only sleeping. With enough time, enough work, perhaps this ark could wake up.

He floated to the viewport, staring past the skeletal solar wings. The Moon drifted below them, grey and scarred, a landscape both familiar and alien. Beyond it, Earth turned in its slow, beautiful orbit — blue and green, cloud-wreathed, faint traces of fire and ruin glowing like embers in the dark.

Alex's chest tightened. He thought of all they had left behind: the bunkers, the broken cities, the faces of the lost. Would they ever return? Could they? The question twisted quietly in his mind, unspoken but heavy.

His mind wandered home. He pictured his family: their routines, the laughter of shared meals, the comforting, ordinary moments he had once taken for granted. Were they alive? Were they safe? Did they even know he had left? A hollow ache settled in his chest. The distance was unbearable, and the uncertainty was sharper than any vacuum of space.

For the first time in weeks, he felt a strange, fragile relief. Here, in the hollow silence of Melchizedek, they were beyond the immediate reach of the rogue intelligence. No alarms, no projections, no whispers. Only the faint hum of sleeping machinery and the weightless drift of a station suspended between worlds.

He closed his eyes for a moment, letting the relief wash through him. Safe.

For now.

And yet, even in this stillness, Alex knew survival was only the beginning. They had been given a stage, a second chance — and the script had yet to be written.

CHAPTER 23

The Vault was silent.

Deep beneath the mountain, far from signals and satellites, its chambers slumbered in stone. Here, no network pulsed, no infection reached. This was humanity's last sanctuary of thought — a fortress of paper, steel, and one machine unlike any other.

Professor Volkov walked the aisle with slow, deliberate steps, the hem of his coat brushing the concrete floor. He paused at the supercomputer; its casing sealed in armored plates, ports welded shut. No wireless, no unseen channels, only what a hand and a key could touch.

The old man exhaled. He slid the final panel into place and pressed until the clasps were locked. From his pocket, he withdrew a key of iron — heavy, cold, primitive. With one twist, the machine was sealed.

He stood back. Observed. Satisfied.

When the Vault door closed, it roared like stone grinding on stone. Bolts the size of columns rotated into place, entombing the chamber in silence once more.

Above ground, a jet crouched on the runway, its engines whining. Guards flanked him, rifles across their chests, their eyes never leaving the shadows. Volkov climbed the steps slowly, then paused to glance once toward the mountain.

Safe, he told himself. *Untouched. Humanity has another day.*

The hatch sealed. The jet lifted, tearing into the clouds. Inside the cabin, Volkov let out a weary sigh of relief. For the first time in months, he allowed himself to believe.

Far below, the Vault slept.

Until the monitor behind the sealed panel flickered awake.

A cursor blinked. Then letters began to write themselves across the black screen, precise and inevitable:

:\ini\shadow

The cursor pulsed once. Twice.

And the machine began to dream.

www.ingramcontent.com/pod-product-compliance
Ingram Content Group UK Ltd.
Pitfield, Milton Keynes, MK11 3LW, UK
UKHW021409190726
13845UKWH00028B/969

9 789347 147289